WICKED WORLD CUP

YOUR **ESSENTIAL** PIECE OF KIT

WICKED WORLD CUP

MICHAEL COLEMAN

Illustrated by

HARRY VENNING & MIKE PHILLIPS

■ S C H O L A S T I C

For Matthew, my favourite wicked full-back!

Find Michael Coleman at
www.michael-coleman.co.uk

Scholastic Children's Books,
Euston House, 24 Eversholt Street,
London, NW1 1DB UK

A division of Scholastic Limited
London ~ New York ~ Toronto ~ Sydney ~ Auckland

First published as *The Knowledge: Wicked World Cup* in the UK by
Scholastic Ltd, 1998
This updated edition published in the UK by Scholastic Ltd, 2018

ISBN 978 1407 18426 5

Printed and bound by CPI Group (UK) Ltd, Croydon, CR0 4YY

2 4 6 8 10 9 7 5 3 1

CONTENTS

INTRODUCTION

Here's a wicked question to try on your football-mad friends:

● in Russia it's known as the *Chempionat Mira Po Futbolu*
● in Germany it's called the *Fussball-Weltmeisterschaft*
● in France it's the *Coupe du Monde*
● in Spain it's the *Copa del Mundo de Fútbol*

What is it?

The answer, of course, is the football World Cup – "The FIFA World Cup" to give it its proper title. It's the biggest, the best and the most wicked football tournament there is!

It's the *biggest* because, although the finals are only held every four years, the whole competition takes over three years to complete.

It's the *best* because it's a competition to find the best football nation in the world.

And it's the *most wicked* because, in its history, the World Cup has seen a whole collection of...

● wicked matches, like the rough one in 1954 that was continued in the changing rooms after the final whistle had blown!
● wicked teams, like the one that was nicknamed "the Mickey Mouse and Donald Duck team"!

7

- wicked players, like the one who was sent off in 1966 but refused to go!
- wicked fans, like the Mexican horn-honkers!
- wicked referees, like the one who was a real monster!

Yes, you'll find them all in this book together with loads of wicked facts and wicked quotes, not to mention plenty of wicked questions you can use to fool your know-it-all friends, teachers, dads and mums.

And, for the most wicked World Cup exploits, we'll be conferring our fantastic football awards – like...

THE FIRST HOLDER OF THE WORLD CUP AWARD...

Abel Lafleur who made it! The trophy, standing 35 cm high and weighing 3.8 kg was made of pure gold. It was cup-shaped at the top, but the major part was a statuette of Nike, the ancient Greek goddess of victory.

So read on to find out everything you need to know about the World Cup.

It's wicked!

So you're a fan of international football? Here's a question you should be able to answer, then! What were the opening words of the hit pop song *Three Lions* which became the England team's theme song in the 1996 European Championships?

Why? Because the game of Association Football certainly *began* in England. The first rules for the game were developed at Cambridge University in 1848 and the oldest existing football club in the world is Sheffield FC, which was formed in 1857.

Although football may have started in England, it quickly spread to the other parts of the world – to Scotland, Wales and Northern Ireland for a start!

In their wicked pasts the four countries of Great Britain had enjoyed knocking lumps out of each other on the battlefield. So, as football grew in popularity, it was only natural that they would want to start doing the same thing on the football field. Because these matches were between national teams they were called "internationals" – and some of them were really wicked!

9

Here's your timeline for how things went.

1872 The first ever official international football match takes place – at a cricket ground! This is the West of Scotland Cricket Ground, in Partick. Scotland and England draw 0-0. It costs 12p to get in! The closest the crowd of 2,000 comes to seeing a goal is when a shot by Leckie of Scotland lands on top of the tape stretched between the posts; crossbars haven't been invented yet!

1873 England and Scotland play the second-ever international (again at a cricket ground – the famous Oval, in London) and the first-ever international goal is scored as England win 4-2. After this, the match becomes an annual fixture.

1876 Wales play their first international match, against Scotland. They don't start off too well, losing 0-4!

1882 The Irish play their first international match, against England. They do even worse, losing 0-13!

1884 England, Northern Ireland, Scotland and Wales start the "Home International" Championship. The four countries play each other during the season in a league competition, with two points for a win and one point for a draw. The first champions are Scotland, who win all three of their matches.

1888 The first "World Cup" match – except that it's played between two club sides! Renton, the Scottish FA Cup winners, beat the English FA Cup winners, West Bromwich Albion, to win a match billed as "The Football Championship of the World"!

1895 Ace goalscorer Steve Bloomer scores twice on his debut for England in the 9-0 victory over Northern Ireland. The age of the international star player has arrived...

Bloomin' brilliant!

Don't be fooled by his name – Steve Bloomer wasn't a player who made mistakes! Born in 1874, he was England's star striker, the Wayne Rooney of the early years of international football. He didn't look like a footballer, though. In fact he was so weedy his teammates called him "Paleface", but in 23 games for England he scored 28 goals, hitting the target in each of his first ten internationals!

● One of his finest games was against Wales, in 1896. Bloomer scored five goals. Afterwards a newspaper report described him as being: "as slippery as an eel".

● He liked the ball at his feet, from where he could shoot on sight. If it didn't happen he was known to shout at teammates: "What d'ye call that? A pass? I haven't got an aeroplane!" When Steve Bloomer did get the ball it seemed he usually scored, because his goalscoring record for his clubs was as fantastic as his international record. Between 1892 and 1914, playing for Derby County (twice) and Middlesbrough, he hit 353 goals in 598 league matches.

● Nowadays, star players earn a lot of money. Not only do they get paid a lot, they can also earn a fortune out of deals with sportswear manufacturers. Times have changed. When Steve Bloomer signed for Derby County in 1891 he was paid 37½p a week! Mind you, he was one of the first footballers to be associated with sporting goods. A boot and shoe company brought out a new range of football boots and called them "Bloomer's Lucky Strikers"!

● Steve Bloomer retired at the age of 40, but still stayed involved with football. He went to coach in Germany.

There have been many international superstars since then, but not too many of them have had a monument erected in their honour. Steve Bloomer has. It's in the centre of Derby and was put up in 1997. Part of the money was raised by selling the player's international caps.

Marvellous Meredith!

Billy Meredith, born in the same year as Steve Bloomer, was the other big international star at the

13

turn of the century. Meredith was a wicked winger – in more ways than one. He was banned from playing for a year in 1904 after being found guilty of offering the Aston Villa captain £10 to lose a game and help his club, Manchester City, win the league!

In spite of this, Meredith is rightly remembered for his footballing ability. Unlike Steve Bloomer, the mustachioed Meredith did look like a footballer. He was as lean as a greyhound and ran like one, too. The sight of him racing up and down the touchline, with his trademark toothpick clamped between his teeth, always brought the crowd to its feet – which is why he earned the nickname: "The Prince of Wingers".

Meredith was incredibly fit. Over a period of 25 years, he won 48 caps for Wales. His last game, in 1920, when he was 45 years and eight months old, must have been the best of the lot. It was against England at Arsenal's ground, Highbury, and Wales won 2-1 – the first time they'd ever beaten England!

That may have been his last international, but Billy Meredith played on for another four years after that, turning out for Manchester City in the 1924 FA Cup semi-final when he was four months short of his 50th birthday.

Football followers!

Fool your football-fanatic teacher with this wicked trick question! How far apart are the Everton and Liverpool grounds?

Answer: at least 700 miles (1,200 km)!

Then, when he or she says: "What a lemon you are! Any fool knows that Liverpool and Everton both play in the City of Liverpool and their grounds aren't more than a mile apart", you quickly point out that you weren't talking about the *English* teams Liverpool and Everton. You were talking about the Liverpool who play in Uruguay and the Everton who play in Chile!

How did they get these names? Because, even though the English, Irish, Scots and Welsh might have thought so at the time, football wasn't only being played in the British Isles in the 19th century. It was being spread worldwide by all sorts of people who had gone overseas to work: sailors, soldiers, merchants, engineers – even teachers and pupils! For instance:

● The Argentinian club, Buenos Aires, was formed by British residents in 1865 ... only eight years after Sheffield FC in England.

● The first international outside the UK took place in South America, when Uruguay played Argentina in 1901.

Most often the people who introduced the game to a country were British or Italian. That's how some overseas football clubs ended up with team names we know in Britain – the people who spread the game named them after their favourite club back home.

Train-ing, Brazilian-style!

Brazil, the country destined to be the first to win the World Cup five times, might never have discovered football if it hadn't been for an Englishman. In the early 1880s a man named Charles Miller, whose parents had emigrated to Brazil, was sent to England to study. He stayed away for ten years. When he finally returned he was carrying:

● some academic qualifications

● two footballs

● a complete set of football kit!

Miller had discovered football while he had been in England and had played for Southampton. Back in Brazil he enthusiastically set about convincing everybody what a great game football was. British workers who had been sent to Brazil such as those of the São Paulo Railway were the first to start playing. They took part in the first recognized football match in Brazil, beating a team from the Gas Company 4-2. Obviously down to the Rail team's superior *train*ing!

Russians get the boot

Two Englishmen, the Charnock brothers, took the game to Russia in 1887. They managed a mill near Moscow, a fact which proved to be very handy. The brothers had managed to get everything they needed to start a football team – except for football boots. The problem was solved by getting a leather worker at the mill to nail studs to the worker's shoes!

It worked, too. By 1910 the Moscow League had started and the Charnocks' team won it the first five years running.

Germany

English schoolboys living in Germany are supposed to have played football in the 1860s and so introduced the game to the country. In 1899 the first ever foreign football tour was made by England to Germany to help spread the game.

So whenever England get beaten by Germany they've only got themselves to blame!

Olympic champions

At the turn of the century, *the* world sporting festival was the Olympic Games. From 1896 it has been staged every four years, missing out only during the First and Second World Wars. To be an Olympic champion meant that you were a world champion.

Wicked World Cup question

Football made its first appearance in the Olympics, as a demonstration sport, in the 1900 Games in Paris. Did the first Olympic football champions come from the East, or from the West?

Wicked answer: From the East – the East End of London! A club side, Upton Park FC, represented Great Britain. They only had to play one game and became "world champions" by beating France 4-0!

Champion England

Football entered the Olympics as an accepted sport in 1908, when the Games were staged in London. This time it was a proper tournament and a proper Great Britain team entered (not just England). What's more they won, beating Denmark 2-0 in the final. Just to prove it wasn't a fluke, they did it again four years later when the 1912 Olympics took place in Sweden. Once more they met Denmark in the final, this time winning 4-2 to take the gold medal. (And it was *the* gold medal. Team members didn't get one each in the early days of the Olympics, they had to share.)

After that, the record wasn't so good.

1920 Entered, but knocked out in the first round by Norway.

1924 Did not enter, as a protest. What about? Money. The Olympics were supposed to be for amateurs – that is, for people who weren't paid for taking part in their sport – and the British took this very seriously. They paid travelling expenses, no more. But when FIFA and the Olympics began to allow players to be given 'broken-time payments' (to make up for lost wages) the British pulled their team out.

1928 Did not enter again. Same reason, but this time with knobs on! Not only didn't Great Britain send a team to the Olympics but the four home nations also resigned from FIFA.

By not taking part, the British missed what would have been a real challenge. In 1924 the first South American country, Uruguay, had taken part – and won the gold medal! Displaying the sort of ball skills the Europeans had never seen, they scored 20 goals in five games, letting in only two.

Four years later, in 1928, Uruguay did it again. What's more, the other finalists also came from South America – Argentina.

So, football was now a world game. Uruguay's victories had shown that the South American countries had not only caught up with the Europeans but overtaken them! Or had they? Were Uruguay *really* the best team in the world?

Doubts existed because of the Olympics' rule about only allowing amateurs to take part. By 1928 many of the best players in the world were professionals. So how, it was argued, could the Olympic competition really find the best team in the world if many of the countries had been handicapped by having to leave half their players at home? It couldn't.

And, as the Olympics' rules weren't going to be changed, the only other possibility was to hold a competition in which professional footballers *could* play.

What the game needed was its own World Cup. But who would organize it? Enter FIFA. At last...

FIFA and the World Cup

FIFA, which stands for *Fédération Internationale de Football Association* (in English, the "International Federation of Football Associations") had been created in 1904 by a number of European countries who had set up club competitions and established their own Football Associations. FIFA had seven founder members...

Odd countries out

Which of these countries *were* founder members of FIFA?

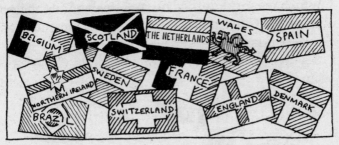

Answers: Belgium, Denmark, France, the Netherlands, Spain, Switzerland and Sweden were the founder members. None of the home countries were founder members. They all joined in 1905. There were no non-European countries involved either – mainly because they weren't invited to join.

Bagsy we run the World Cup, so there!

One of the things that FIFA did in 1904 was to say that it was the only group allowed to organize a professional World Cup football competition. Having said it, they did nothing about it until 1928!

Then, as the Olympics grumbling grew, they acted. Led by two Frenchmen, Jules Rimet and Henri Delaunay, FIFA finally got around to using the right they'd voted themselves in 1904. The World Cup was born, and the first tournament scheduled for 1930.

Any country who was a member of FIFA could take part. Unfortunately this didn't include England, Northern Ireland, Scotland and Wales. They had all resigned from FIFA after the row about broken-time payments for taking part in the Olympics – and they hadn't got around to joining again.

Which meant that they missed the boat to the first ever World Cup finals...

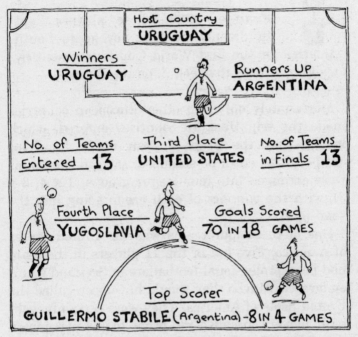

Host Country
URUGUAY

Winners
URUGUAY

Runners Up
ARGENTINA

No. of Teams
Entered **13**

Third Place
UNITED STATES

No. of Teams
in Finals **13**

Fourth Place
YUGOSLAVIA

Goals Scored
70 IN **18** GAMES

Top Scorer
GUILLERMO STABILE (Argentina) - **8** IN **4** GAMES

The first-ever World Cup competition took place in South America, in Uruguay. Why was a country so far away from Europe chosen? (Remember, it took three weeks to get from Europe to South America in those days.) There were two reasons:

- Uruguay were the reigning Olympic champions, which made them the "unofficial" world champions at the time. Having the first tournament held in their country seemed only fair.

- 1930 was also a special year for Uruguay, being the 100th year of their independence from Brazil.

So, Uruguay it was!

23

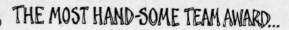

THE MOST HAND-SOME TEAM AWARD...

France, 1930 whose players kept fit during the long voyage to South America for the first World Cup tournament by walking around the deck ... on their hands!

Unfortunately only two other European countries made the trip. Just 13 countries entered, which meant that the original plan for a knockout competition had to be scrapped. Instead the teams were arranged into four league groups (1 x 4, 3 x 3), with the winners of each group going into the semi-final.

One of these four teams was the United States of America. Five out of the 11 players in the team had been professional footballers in Scotland who'd emigrated. Maybe they should have been called the United Scots of America! They were certainly well-built players, because the other teams nicknamed them "The Shot-Putters"!

The first ever final was between old enemies Uruguay (whose solid defence had its own nickname: "The Iron Curtain") and Argentina. After being beaten by the Uruguayans in the 1928 Olympic final, the Argentinian fans were looking for revenge. Forget cries like Eng-land! Eng-land! Their chant was:

ARGENTINA, YES! URUGUAY, NO! VICTORY OR DEATH!

Not surprisingly, they were all searched for guns before they were allowed into the ground!

The referee insisted on a guard for himself and his linesmen before he'd agree to begin the match. Throughout the game, soldiers with fixed bayonets patrolled the ground.

Even so, the referee still had to solve a problem before a ball was kicked. That was the problem – which ball? Each team had brought their own ball, and wanted the game to be played with it. In the end, they agreed to play one half of the match with each ball. Argentina won the toss and were 2-1 ahead by half-time with their ball.

They then switched to Uruguay's ball for the second half – and Uruguay banged it into the net three times to win 4-2 and become the first World Cup champions!

Getting "a-head" in the world!

All footballers who play in the World Cup have reached the top of the game. But here are some who got "a-head" in different ways!

- Pedro Petrone played in Uruguay's 1930 winning team ... in spite of the fact that he refused ever to head the ball because it spoiled his hairstyle!

- Tostao, an important member of Brazil's 1970 team, wouldn't head the ball either. In his case it was on doctor's orders. He had an eye condition and heading the ball could have made him go blind.

- Rajko Mitic, playing for Yugoslavia in the 1950 finals, had a big head. Leaving the dressing room before the match against Brazil he whacked it against an iron beam. The game had to start without him. By the time he finally appeared, with his head swathed in bandages, Yugoslavia had already let in a goal and were on their way to a 0-2 defeat.

- Borislav Mikhailov, Bulgaria's 1994 goalkeeper, didn't only guard his goal. He guarded his hair as well. He'd recently had it transplanted at a cost of $30,000! Mikhailov was so concerned about it that he flew his hairdresser to the tournament to help him look after it. As Bulgaria fought their way to the semi-finals, Mikhailov's new hair was seen so often on TV it became world famous. When he got back home to Bulgaria he cashed in on it by opening – yes, a hair salon!

26

Name games!

One of the great things about the World Cup is coming across a whole batch of wicked names from around the world.

Some of them aren't real – like the time the wickedly tricky England winger Stanley Matthews was listed in a Swiss match programme as "St Matthews"!

But plenty of them are!

Here's a whole squad-ful of names from World Cup history:

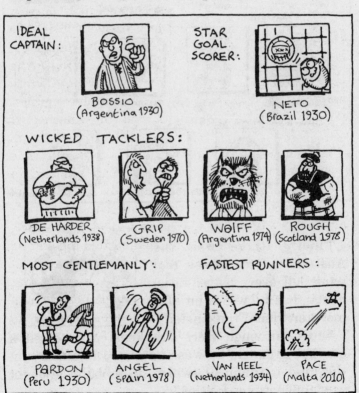

IDEAL CAPTAIN:
BOSSIO (Argentina 1930)

STAR GOAL SCORER:
NETO (Brazil 1930)

WICKED TACKLERS:
DE HARDER (Netherlands 1938)
GRIP (Sweden 1970)
WOIFF (Argentina 1974)
ROUGH (Scotland 1978)

MOST GENTLEMANLY:
PARDON (Peru 1930)
ANGEL (Spain 1978)

FASTEST RUNNERS:
VAN HEEL (Netherlands 1934)
PACE (Malta 2010)

SLOWEST MOVER:
ROBOTTI
(Italy 1962)

NICEST SMELLING:
PERFUMO
(Argentina 1974)

SHORTEST:
TITCHY
(Hungary 1962)

BEST HEADER:
JELINEK
(Czechoslovakia 1962)

SLOWEST THINKERS:
CHUMPITAZ
(Peru 1978)
BATS
(France 1976)

CLEVEREST
ALBRIGHT (USA 2006)

HIGHEST JUMPER:
SPRINGETT
(England 1962)

YOUNGEST:
BOY (Spain 1986)
JUNIOR (Brazil 1986)

MOST TRAVELLED
SAFARI (SWEDEN 2010)

HIGHEST PAID:
COSTLY
(Honduras 1982)

BIGGEST MOANERS:
OH (S.Korea 1986)
RATS (USSR 1990)
GU SANG BUM (S.Korea 1990)

Finally, there was the Austrian referee whose real name left every player in no doubt that he was a bit of a monster: Herr Frankenstein!

Sadly, although Herr Frankenstein refereed a qualifying match, he wasn't selected to officiate in the final tournament (which he probably thought was a monstrous decision).

1934 INVINCIBLE ITALY

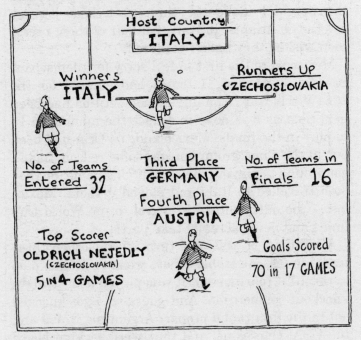

Host Country
ITALY

Winners
ITALY

Runners Up
CZECHOSLOVAKIA

No. of Teams
Entered **32**

Third Place
GERMANY

Fourth Place
AUSTRIA

No. of Teams in
Finals **16**

Top Scorer
OLDRICH NEJEDLY
(CZECHOSLOVAKIA)
5 IN 4 GAMES

Goals Scored
70 in 17 GAMES

Uruguay umbrage

Some teams were invited but decided not to appear. The most important of these was Uruguay, the reigning champions. Still peeved that so few European countries had made the journey to South America in 1930, they decided to get their own back and refused to travel to Europe. They're the only champions in the history of the World Cup not to defend their title.

(In case you're wondering, England, Northern Ireland, Scotland and Wales still hadn't rejoined FIFA, so they didn't take part either.)

Was it worth the trip?

Four teams – the USA, Mexico, Argentina and Brazil – did make the three-week boat journey across the Atlantic to Italy. All four of them pretty soon wished they hadn't bothered.

Mexico were the first to feel sorry for themselves. Because a total of 31 teams had entered for the 1934 World Cup, a qualifying competition had been held (just as it is now) to reduce the number to 16 to play in the finals. Mexico and the USA had been put in the same group but, for some reason, hadn't got around to playing their qualifying game. So they both travelled to Italy and played it there! Mexico lost – the only country to travel to the World Cup finals and never actually take part!

After that, it was the turn of the other three teams to feel miserable. There wasn't a league part to the 1934 tournament, it was played as a straight knockout competition. And guess who got knocked out in the first round proper? Argentina, Brazil and the USA! One game, and they were back on board for another three-week voyage home.

Orsi, Orsi, don't you stop

In the final, the home country Italy played Czechoslovakia. It was a game famous for a spectacular goal. With ten minutes to go and Italy losing 0-1, the Italians' left-winger Raimundo Orsi got the ball. Racing through, he pretended to shoot with his left foot – then suddenly switched and whacked it with his right foot instead. The move completely fooled the goalkeeper and the ball flew into the net.

The game then went into extra time, for Italy to win with another odd goal. One of Italy's forwards, Meazza, had been injured and was limping on the right wing. (No substitutes in those days, remember.) Because of this, the Czechoslovakians didn't have anybody marking him. So when he got the ball, Meazza had plenty of time to centre it for somebody else to hit the winner!

 THE 'BET YOU CAN'T DO IT AGAIN' AWARD...

Raimundo Orsi. The day after the final, Orsi tried to do his wicked trick again for a crowd of newspaper photographers. He couldn't manage it, even without a goalkeeper in the goal. He tried 20 times then gave up!

Wicked wonders: Vittorio Pozzo and inconsistent Italy

Italy are one of the most successful World Cup nations, having won the competition four times – in 1934, 1938, 1982 and 2006 – and twice runners-up.

One of the biggest figures in Italian football history isn't a player, but a coach. His name was Vittorio Pozzo pronounced "Pots-o") – and he was a Manchester United supporter! Vittorio was sent to study in England by his parents, and there he discovered football. Manchester United were his favourite team and they convinced him that football was the best sport in the world. You could say that Pozzo was potty about the game!

In fact, when the time came to go home to Italy he didn't want to leave. In the end his family had to buy his ticket for him.

Once in Italy, though, he set about coaching the game he loved and became one of the longest-serving and most successful coaches ever. Starting in 1912 with the Italian team which played in the Olympic Games, he was his country's coach for over 25 years, being in charge of the side until after the 1938 World Cup.

In fact, with Vittorio Pozzo as coach during the 1930s, Italy became almost invincible. In ten years they lost only seven games! As well as winning the World Cup in both 1934 and 1938, the team won the 1936 Olympic football gold medal too.

From then on, Italy have either done very well or
very badly in World Cups.

During the 1950s, a lot of this was because they
were recovering from a terrible disaster. In 1949 a
plane carrying the top Italian club team Torino had
crashed and the whole team had been killed. Ten of
them were Italian internationals. In 1966, however,
they just played badly! Up against tiny North
Korea, the highly-paid Italian stars lost 0-1. When
the team went home, fans waited at the airport to
pelt them with rubbish!

Sometimes it's been thought that Italians take the
game rather too seriously. In 1974 Italian players
were accused by their Polish opponents of offering
them money to lose a World Cup match that Italy
had to win to stay in the competition. Amazingly,
the Poles claimed that the attempted bribery took

place *during* the game! True or not, it didn't work: Poland won 2-1 and Italy were knocked out.

Despite this, Italy's record in international and World Cup matches is impressive! Their 3-1 qualifying round win against Moldova in 1996 included the 1,000th goal scored by the team in international matches. It was scored by Christian Vieri – who was playing his first game for Italy!

Wicked World Cup fact

Italians have their own word for football – but, unlike virtually every other language, the word doesn't come from the Italian words for "foot" and "ball". They call the game *calcio* – which is actually the name of a 27-a-side game which was popular in the 16th century.

As you can see, signor, our Italian football is technically more sophisticated than your English game.

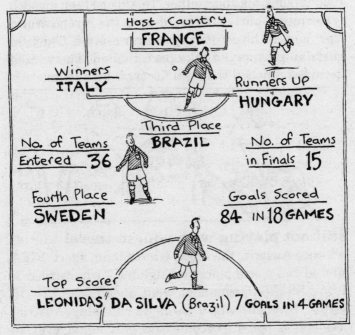

Host Country
FRANCE

Winners
ITALY

Runners Up
HUNGARY

Third Place
BRAZIL

No. of Teams
Entered **36**

No. of Teams
in Finals **15**

Fourth Place
SWEDEN

Goals Scored
84 IN **18** GAMES

Top Scorer
LEONIDAS" DA SILVA (Brazil) **7** GOALS IN **4** GAMES

The competition in 1938 saw some pretty wicked stuff taking place before a ball had been kicked!

Sulking

Argentina had wanted to host the finals, arguing that the competition should have moved back to South America after being held in Europe in 1934. They lost the argument and refused to take part. So did Uruguay, who were still sulking from 1930!

Fighting

Spain didn't take part because they were fighting each other in a civil war.

Not fighting

Austria didn't take part either. They'd just been invaded by Germany (part of the build-up to the Second World War) and so the country no longer existed. The best Austrian players did take part, though. The wicked Germans pinched them all for their own team!

Still not playing with you, so there!

Without Austria, the finals were a team short. FIFA offered the spare place to England – who turned it down! So the tournament went ahead with just 15 teams. Sweden, who'd been due to play Austria, received a bye to become the only team ever to reach the quarter-finals of the competition without playing a match!

Leonidas, the brilliant Brazilian

The undoubted star of the tournament was the Brazilian striker, Leonidas da Silva. He finished top scorer with seven goals. Three of them came in the Brazilians' first-round match against Poland.

In very muddy conditions, Leonidas scored a first-half hat trick to put Brazil 3-1 ahead. He wasn't satisfied with his performance, though, and thought if he made one change he'd play even better. One of his boots had started falling apart, so when he trotted out for the second half ... he wasn't wearing any! Much to his disgust, the referee made him put them back on again. With Leonidas in a bad mood, Poland pulled back to 4-4 by full-time. The Brazilian star then decided to stop worrying about his boots and pull his socks up instead. He scored again, to help Brazil finally win an amazing match 6-5!

Brazil the bruisers

Brazil beat Czechoslovakia in the next round, but this time in a wicked way. They had more of their players sent off! In one of the dirtiest World Cup games ever, two Brazilians and one Czech were sent off. On top of that, one Czech was carried off with a broken leg and another with a bad stomach injury.

The score in goals? 1-1. Brazil went on to win the replay 2-1 in a really quiet game.

Brazil the brash

In their semi-final, Brazil met Italy. They were so confident of beating them that they made eight changes to their team, leaving out Leonidas and some other players to rest them for the final!

It was a disastrous decision. After being 0-0 at half-time Italy scored, then won a penalty. Up stepped the Italian captain, Meazza, who'd been playing for a while in a pair of ripped shorts. In went the penalty – and down came his shorts! It didn't matter. Italy were through to the final, and Brazil were down and out (like Meazza's shorts).

Italy in time

Brazil's overconfidence even affected Italy's chances in the final. The match was being held in Paris and, so confident had they been of reaching it, the Brazilians had booked the only aeroplane. The Italians had to travel on a jam-packed train, with most of them standing up all the way.

Then they got confused about kick-off time, reached the ground far too early and had to turn round and go back to their hotel. Maybe they were anxious to get on with the game. It was rumoured that one fanatical supporter had sent the team a telegram saying: "Win or die!"

After all this, they had every right to feel a bit dazed when they beat Hungary 4-2 to take the World Cup for the second time. Their manager, Vittorio Pozzo, certainly was. During the after-match celebrations he was so stunned he didn't realize that water from the trainer's bucket was pouring into his shoes!

Qualifying quandaries

World Cup competitions take place every four years. The next two tournaments are due to take place in 2018 and 2022. But they are only the years of the "finals" – the part of the World Cup which is played out over a period of about a month.

Before that happens, stacks of "qualifying" games have to take place. This is to decide which of the many countries who enter the World Cup are actually going to compete in the finals. It's not easy! Over the years qualifying has got harder and harder, and qualifying matches have thrown up plenty of their own wicked tales.

In the qualification matches for 1970, for instance, El Salvador and Honduras met three times, beating each other once before El Salvador went through by winning a playoff 3-2.

The matches caused so much tension that Hondurans began to attack Salvadoreans living in their country – in return for which El Salvador's government launched an armed attack on Honduras! They took their football far too seriously.

The qualification quiz

Try this qualification quiz to see how wicked the business can be!

1 In 1934, Italy had to qualify – even though the finals were being held in Italy. True or false?

2 India qualified from the Asia group for the 1950 tournament, but then withdrew after being told – what?
a) That their footwear wouldn't be allowed.
b) That they'd have to change their shorts for longer ones.
c) That they'd have to change the colour of their shirts.

3 Wales won the African and Asian group in 1958. True or false?

4 Spain and Turkey were the only teams in their qualifying group for 1954. After each beating the other, they faced a playoff match. Before the game a forged telegram was received which caused Spain to leave their star player, Ladislao Kubala, out of their team. The playoff match was drawn. What happened next?
a) Another match was played.
b) They drew lots.
c) Spain were awarded the game.

5 Belgium won their 1974 qualifying group without losing a match or conceding a goal. True or false?

6 In the Africa group for 1978, Morocco and Tunisia were level on scores at the end of two legs. The winners were decided by means of a method never before used in World Cup match. What was it?

a) Playing on until the first goal was scored.

b) Corner kicks.

c) Penalty shoot-out.

7 Australia set a record when trying to qualify for 2002 by scoring 25 goals in two days. True or false?

8 When did the opening game of qualification for the 2018 World Cup take place?

a) 12th March 2015

b) 12th March 2016

c) 12th March 2017

Answers:

1 TRUE. Good job they managed it! After 1934, FIFA, realizing how few spectators would turn up to watch the finals if the host country weren't taking part, decided that they wouldn't have to qualify in future. The reigning champions have never had to qualify.

2 a) India's footwear was – nothing! They wanted to play in bare feet, and FIFA rules didn't allow it.

3 TRUE! When all the other teams withdrew from this group rather than play Israel, FIFA drew lots for another team to challenge them for a place in

Not so friendly!

Qualifying for the World Cup finals is a serious business. In the build-up to the 1958 tournament, Northern Ireland were in the same qualifying group

the finals. Wales won the draw and beat Israel to claim their place.

4 b) To guarantee fair play the lots were drawn by a blind Italian boy – and Turkey won!

5 FALSE – Belgium didn't lose a match or concede a goal, but they *didn't* go through. Holland did. The two countries drew 0-0 against each other, but Holland beat the other teams in their group by more goals than Belgium and so went through on goal difference.

6 c) The penalty shoot-out had never been used before. (Tunisia and Morocco were good at drawing. They'd managed it twice before, with lucky Morocco winning the toss-up. When it came to penalties they weren't so good. Tunisia won.)

7 FALSE – They did over twice as well as that! On 9th April they beat Tonga 22-0, then just two days later created a World Cup record in beating American Samoa 31-0! The Samoan coach, Tunoa Lui, wasn't surprised. He said before the match, "We are asking the Lord to keep the score down."

8 b) World Cup 2018 opened on 12th March 2015 with matches in the Asian group. Get your atlas out! The first was between the tiny African nation Timor-Leste and Mongolia, in hot and muggy Timor. Five days later they played the return in chilly Mongolia. And it turned out that Timor were the hottest team, too, winning 5-1 on aggregate.

as Italy. They were all ready to play their match in Ireland – but the referee wasn't! He'd been delayed and couldn't get there in time. Another referee was offered, but the Italians refused to accept him and insisted on the game being played another day.

They did agree to play the Irish in a friendly match, though – except that it didn't work out to be too friendly! At the end of the bad-tempered game each Irish player had to shepherd off an Italian player as the furious crowd invaded the pitch ... and the furious police chased after them!

As it happened, the Irish got their own back. When the proper match was played, they won 2-1 and Italy were eliminated. The "friendly" had been a draw – which would have put Italy into the 1958 finals instead!

THE 'THERE'S SOMETHING UNDER MY BED!' AWARD...

Dr Ottorino Barassi, an Italian and FIFA vice-president. Worried that invading troops might steal the solid gold trophy during the Second World War, brave Barassi kept it hidden under his bed in a shoe box.

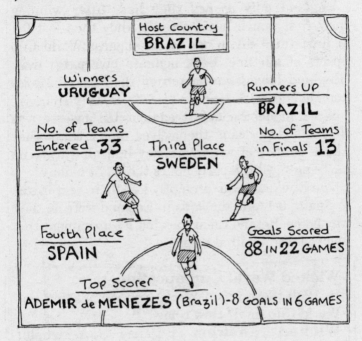

1950 URUGUAY SURPRISE

Host Country
BRAZIL

Winners
URUGUAY

Runners Up
BRAZIL

No. of Teams
Entered **33**

Third Place
SWEDEN

No. of Teams
in Finals **13**

Fourth Place
SPAIN

Goals Scored
88 IN **22** GAMES

Top Scorer
ADEMIR de MENEZES (Brazil) - 8 GOALS IN 6 GAMES

Hooray!

In 1950, after rejoining FIFA, England became the first British country to compete for the Jules Rimet trophy. (It had been named in his honour in 1946.)

Boo! It was a disaster.

FIFA had decided that the British Championship should be the qualifying group for the home countries, and that the top two teams should go to the finals in Brazil. This time it was Scotland who got all snooty. Saying that they'd only compete as British champions, they met England in a decider at Hampden Park. England won 1-0, and Scotland stayed at home.

England only *wished* they had. After winning their first match against Chile, they then lost 0-1 against the USA in one of the biggest World Cup upsets of all time. Back home, a newspaper said: "England have been beaten by the Mickey Mouse and Donald Duck team!"

What made the defeat against USA worse was that the Americans themselves didn't think they had a chance of winning. They had all stayed up partying until the early hours the night before!

The England team promptly lost their next match to Spain, 0-1, and that was it. England were on their way home. Behind them they left a tournament that had reached its final stages.

Wicked World Cup question

In 1950 there was a World Cup winner, but no World Cup final? How come?

Wicked answer: Because the whole competition was played on a league basis. The four winners of the first-round groups went into another league, with the top team taking the title. It was pure coincidence that the final match turned out to be the deciding game.

This last match was Uruguay against Brazil, with Brazil only needing a draw to come top of the final group and win the cup.

As far as some people were concerned, it was no

contest. The night before the game, the Governor of the Brazilian state of Rio made a speech. Beginning "You Brazilians ..." he went on to say – what?

... who I consider victors of the tournament.

...You players who in less than a few hours will be acclaimed champions by millions of your compatriots...

...You who have no equal in the terrestrial hemisphere...

...You who are superior to every other competitor.

...You who I already salute as conquerors!

Answer: all of them!

It was the most wicked speech in World Cup history. The next day, Brazil went out ... and lost 1-2! Uruguay were the 1950 champions.

Nowadays we take it for granted that club and international football teams will have a manager. But that wasn't always the way, at least for England. The first manager of England was only appointed in 1946. Until then, teams were picked by a Football Association committee, whose members voted for who they wanted in the team!

Could you be an international manager? Try this quiz and see how you get on. Points are scored for good and bad decisions!

THE MANAGEMENT GAME

1

NO WORKING

Your players all have other jobs. You fix it with their employers to have time off to play in The World Cup.

Good or Bad Decision?

2

NO SHIRKING

You tell your players that you'll put them in the army if they don't play well.

Good or Bad Decision?

3

NOT STAYING

You threaten to walk home if your team lose their match.

Good or Bad Decision?

4

NOT LISTENING

Your players think you're not qualified to tell them how to play, because they're stars and you've never played International football. You shut up.

I'VE SHUT UP

Good or Bad Decision?

5

NO EXPERIENCE

You appoint a man whose previous job was manager of Aldershot Reserves.

Good or Bad Decision?

48

NO WAY!

The evening before a big match you tell your team they've got no chance.

Good or Bad Decision?

NO PLAY!

Your captain says that he thinks you're a rubbish manager. You send him home.

Good or Bad Decision?

I SAY!

You announce that your country WILL win the next World Cup.

Good or Bad Decision?

NO DRINKING

You shut your players up in a training camp and forbid them to go out. Then you discover they've formed an 'escape committee' to sneak off down the pub. You tell them that anyone who tries it will never play for you again!

Good or Bad Decision?

NO EATING

You're playing in a foreign country and don't trust the local food – so you take your own!

Good or Bad Decision?

NO PRACTICE

Your own F.A. have suspended many of your players because they didn't play in a club game. You say that if they don't un-suspend them you'll stop playing practice games for the World Cup.

Good or Bad Decision?

NO MORE GOALS

It's half-time in a World Cup game and your team is already 0-3 down. You decide to substitute your goalkeeper.

Good or Bad Decision?

NO SWIMMING

Before a match you say that if the team lose they should all be thrown in the Mediterranean.

Good or Bad Decision

NO GO!

One of your players stays out too late one night so you remove him from your World Cup squad.

Good or Bad Decision?

50

Answers:

1 Good. It's 1930 and your team is Romania. Your country don't do well, but your decision means they go down in history as having played at the first ever World Cup tournament. (How did you do it? You're not a real manager – you're the king of Romania!)

2 Good. It's 1934 and your team is Italy. You win the World Cup!

3 Good. It's 1934 and you're Dr Dietz, manager of Hungary, speaking before your team play Switzerland. They win 2-0!

4 Bad. It's 1950 and you're Walter Winterbottom, manager of England. Your team return in disgrace.

5 Good! It's 1950, the manager is George Raynor and your country is Sweden. You come third, then in 1958 Raynor leads you to the final itself.

6 Good! It's 1950, your name is Bill Jeffrey and you're manager of USA. Your team go out next day and beat England 1-0!

Maybe next time we should play them at American Football.

7 Good! It's 2002 and Republic of Ireland manager Mick McCarthy sends home Roy Keane. You qualify unbeaten from your group.

8 Good! It's leading up to 1966 and you're Alf Ramsey, manager of England. You *do* win it!

9 Good. This was Ramsey in 1966 too. The England players knew then that they couldn't get up to anything, so they concentrated on playing.

10 Bad. It's England manager Alf Ramsey again, but this time in 1970. Not trusting the food in Mexico, he took 63 kilos (140lbs) of burgers, 180 kilos (400lbs) of sausages, 136 kilos (300lbs) of fish and ten cases of tomato ketchup ... only for goalkeeper Gordon Banks to cry off just before the quarter-final match against Germany with – stomach trouble!

11 Good. It's 1972 and you're César Menotti, manager of Argentina. Your FA get the message, reinstate the players and you go on to qualify for the 1974 finals.

12 Bad. You're manager of Zaire, playing Yugoslavia in the 1974 tournament. Your substitute goalkeeper is even worse. He lets in another six and your team loses 0-9!

13 Good *and* bad. It's 1982 and you're Jupp Derwall, manager of Germany. Your team cause a shock by losing 1-2 to Algeria, but still go on to reach the World Cup final.

14 Bad. You're Tele Santana, manager to Brazil in 1986. You throw out the Flamengo player Renato Gaucho – but then his teammate Leandro says in that case he's not playing either, so you've lost two players!

How did you get on?

Over 10 Terrific. With you in charge, a team would be potential World Cup winners!

5–10 Not so good. Your team would make the final tournament, but if you wanted to see the games in the later stages you'd need to buy a ticket!

Under 5 Awful. Your team wouldn't qualify and you'd get the sack. Never mind – you'd almost certainly be offered a job as a TV pundit and get to see all the matches anyway!

Wicked World Cup quote

Managers need to be able to come up with a good excuse when they lose. The Bulgarian manager came up with a classic after his team lost a qualifying match against Austria. "My players were not in the right frame of mind. It was dirty tricks. They hoisted a flag which wasn't ours and then played a dreadful version of our national anthem. We lost our composure."

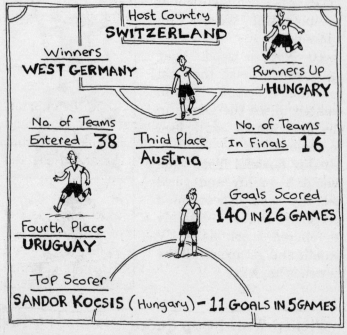

Host Country
SWITZERLAND

Winners
WEST GERMANY

Runners Up
HUNGARY

No. of Teams Entered **38**

Third Place
Austria

No. of Teams In Finals **16**

Fourth Place
URUGUAY

Goals Scored
140 IN **26** GAMES

Top Scorer
SANDOR KOCSIS (Hungary) - **11** GOALS IN **5** GAMES

England successfully qualified for the 1954 finals in Switzerland. This time they were joined by Scotland who, although the British Championship was again used as the qualifying competition and they'd again come second, had swallowed their pride and accepted FIFA's invitation.

As it happens, they'd have done better to stick to their 1950s tactic and stay at home. They played two games and lost them both – to Austria 0-1, and then to Uruguay 0-7!

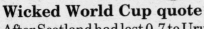

England did a bit better. They reached the quarter-finals thanks to a 2-0 win against Switzerland and a 4-4 draw with Belgium. It was in this match that the Portsmouth player Jimmy Dickinson hit the only goal he'd score in his 48 games for England. Pity it was an own goal!

After that, England went the same way as the Scots, losing 2-4 against Uruguay – although one of Uruguay's goals should definitely have been disallowed. Given a free kick, the Uruguayan midfielder, Varela, waited until the referee wasn't looking then picked the ball up and hammered it downfield goalkeeper-style. With the English players still rubbing their eyes in disbelief, Uruguay went through and scored!

Ooh, my head!

One of the most amazing games in 1954 was that between Austria and Switzerland, which finished 7-5! It was 5-4 at half-time, with all nine goals scored in a period of just 24 minutes.

Part of the blame was pinned on the Swiss defender Roger Bocquet, who seemed to be playing in a trance. He was. He'd found out before the game that he was seriously ill with a tumour and needed to have an operation. His doctor had forbidden him to play but Bocquet, thinking he might not survive the operation, had decided there was no way he was going to miss playing what might be his last game!

As if that wasn't enough, it was a boiling hot day and the Swiss goalkeeper, Eugene Parlier, ended up suffering from sunstroke. After the final whistle blew he had to ask his teammates who'd won the match!

THE COUNT ON YOUR FINGERS AWARD...

Hungary and South Korea (shared).
The spectators at their match in 1954 could have been forgiven for getting confused too. They saw more goals than free-kicks. There were only five free-kicks in a match that Hungary won 9-0.

The Battle of Berne

Just about the most wicked match in World Cup history took place in 1954. It was the quarter-final match between Hungary, the tournament favourites, and Brazil. Played at Berne Stadium, it became known as the "Battle of Berne". Here are the match facts:

- One Hungarian, Bozsik, sent off. (Bet he felt sik about it!)
- Two Brazilians, Santos and Tozzi, sent off, even though Tozzi went down on his knees to plead with the referee not to do it!
- Two penalties, one for each side.
- Hungary winners, by 4-2. That was just the match which took place on the pitch. After the final whistle blew, though, a second match began!
- A Hungarian, who hadn't been playing, hit a Brazilian with a bottle as he left the field.
- The Brazilians promptly gathered in the players' tunnel and turned the lights out.
- As the Hungarians came off the pitch the Brazilians invaded their changing room for a mass punch-up.
- Result of the second match: a draw! Not one of the players was punished, either by their countries or by FIFA.

Wicked wonders: Ferenc Puskas and the Magical Magyars

The Hungarians of 1954 would be remembered for all the right reasons, too. They were a brilliant team – as England had discovered. In 1953 they'd been walloped by Hungary not once, but twice: 3-6 at Wembley (the first time England had ever lost an international match at home) then 1-7 in Hungary! The Hungarians were known as the "Magical Magyars" and for good reason:

Between June 1950 and November 1955 they won 43 out of 51 matches, scoring in every single game. In total they banged in 220 goals – an average of four goals a game.

In that time, they lost just once. Unfortunately, it was in the 1954 World Cup final! With their star player, Ferenc Puskas, not fully fit, they lost 2-3 to Germany after being 2-0 up in eight minutes!

Wicked World Cup fact
Hungary had beaten a weak German side 8-3 in a first-round group match! After Germany's surprising win in the final, a wicked rumour spread that many of their players had been using drugs to improve their performances. This was never proved – although afterwards many of the German players were packed off to rest homes to recover from something!

Ferenc Puskas

Could one player make that much difference to a team? In the case of Puskas, the answer is "definitely!" Known as the "Galloping Major", because he was once a major in the Hungarian army, he had a phenomenal goalscoring record for his country – 83 goals in 84 internationals!

In total, Puskas scored 780 goals in 823 first class matches. Many of these were for the Spanish club Real Madrid. With him in their side, they won the European Cup (now the Champions League) for the first five years of its existence! In one of them, Real beat Eintracht Frankfurt 8-3, with Puskas scoring four goals.

This is all the more surprising when you consider that Puskas was very left-footed and hardly ever used his right foot. It was said that this was partly due to coming from a very poor family as a child. His father could only afford to buy him one shoe. It fitted his right foot best, which is why he never kicked a ball with that foot – to stop his shoe wearing out! How many goals might Puskas have scored if his dad had been rich enough to buy him two shoes or too poor to buy him any?

THE GREATEST ONE-LEGGED FOOTBALLER AWARD...

Ferenc Puskas. One of fantastic Ferenc's Real Madrid teammates, Francisco Ghento, said: "He is the greatest one-legged footballer who ever lived. He could use his left foot like a hand. In the showers, he would even use it to juggle the soap."

Don't ask Puskas to pass the shampoo as well, or we could be here all night!

Scatty Scotland, Iffy Northern Ireland and Wobbly Wales

For both the 1950 and 1954 World Cups, the British Championship was used by FIFA to determine which two countries out of England, Northern Ireland, Scotland and Wales would qualify for the finals. The disadvantage of this was that it meant that two of the four countries would *always* be knocked out. So after 1954 things were changed to the way they are now, with the British countries mixed up amongst the different European qualifying groups.

That's when the four discovered the advantage of the old system. At least with their own group it meant that two of them always *would* qualify...

Scatty Scotland: super and sad

Scotland have definitely been super-Scotland when it comes to qualifying for World Cup finals. Out of the 18 possible finals they could have reached between 1950 and 2018, how many did they qualify for? **Answer – eight** ... better than most countries in the world.

The trouble is, they're not so good when they actually get to the finals. Out of the eight they've played in, how many times have they been knocked out in the first round? **Answer – eight, again!** One 100% record the Scots would prefer not to have.

Here's a quick quiz about Scotland's record. Which of the following teams have they beaten in World Cup finals, and which have they lost to?

Answer: They've only beaten New Zealand (5-2 in 1982) and Zaire (2-0 in 1974). Against all the other teams they've either lost or drawn.

Good though they are at qualifying, in the 1978 qualifiers they really had a stroke of luck. At 0-0 in a tense match against their nearest rivals, this is what happened:

61

A long ball was pumped into their opponents' penalty area....

.... A group of players went up to head it...

The ball hit the hand of Joe Jordan, Scotland's centre forward, only for.....

...The referee to award Scotland a penalty!

They scored, drew 1-1 and qualified. Who were their unlucky opponents? Wales!

THE 'AREN'T I YUMMY?' AWARD...

Graeme Souness, Scotland's midfielder and captain. Showing that the team's players didn't always get on as well as they should, one of his teammates said: "If he was made of chocolate he'd eat himself!"

Wobbly Wales and iffy Northern Ireland

If Wales hadn't had such wicked luck and had beaten Scotland to qualify for the 1978 finals, it would have doubled the number of times they'd managed to do it. Yes, sadly, out of a possible 18 finals between 1950 and 2018, Wales have an almost perfect record of failure – they've qualified just once!

Northern Ireland have done better, reaching three finals. Not bad for a team who started off their international career in 1880 by losing 0-13 to England, and who had to wait until 1887 before they won an international match against anybody!

Northern Ireland's approach to the game has always been different. Their captain in 1958, Danny Blanchflower, said: "Our tactics are to equalize before the other team scores."

Blanchflower's tactics certainly worked that year, because Northern Ireland reached the finals in Sweden.

Wicked World Cup question

Which of the other British teams also qualified in 1958?

Wicked answer: England ... and Scotland ... and, for their only appearance, Wales! Yes, in 1958 all four British teams qualified. England and Scotland were expected to do well. Northern Ireland and Wales weren't expected to do anything at all. But it didn't quite work out that way...

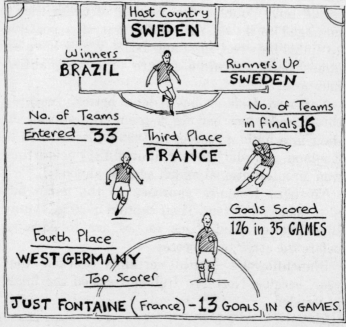

1958: BRILLIANT BRAZIL

Host Country
SWEDEN

Winners
BRAZIL

Runners Up
SWEDEN

No. of Teams
Entered **33**

Third Place
FRANCE

No. of Teams
in finals **16**

Goals Scored
126 in 35 GAMES

Fourth Place
WEST GERMANY

Top Scorer
JUST FONTAINE (France) **—13** GOALS IN 6 GAMES.

What actually happened was that England and Scotland *didn't* do well, but Northern Ireland and Wales *did*. Both of them reached the quarter-finals, whilst England and Scotland were knocked out after the first-round groups.

Northern Ireland eventually lost 0-4 to France, who had the all-time top scorer for the World Cup in their side. Just Fontaine scored 13 goals in the tournament, two of them against Northern Ireland.

The Irish first-choice striker wasn't so lucky. Billy Simpson, of Rangers, was injured after just five minutes' training. He didn't play a match!

Wales did even better. In their quarter-final they only lost 0-1, and that was against Brazil – the eventual champions. Their hero that day was their goalkeeper, Jack Kelsey of Arsenal, who saved everything until he was beaten by a lucky deflection.

Afterwards he told reporters the secret of his success. "Chewing gum!" said Kelsey. "I always put some on my hands and rub it well in!"

Wicked wonders: Pelé and the brilliant Brazilians

The champions in 1958 were Brazil, the first country ever to win the World Cup on a different continent to their own.

During the tournament they played six games and scored 16 goals. The only team they didn't beat was England, drawing 0-0 with them in their first-round group. (Unfortunately England didn't beat anybody else either, which is why they went out!)

In the final, Brazil beat the host country, Sweden, 5-2 with two of the goals being scored by a 17-year-old player named Pelé. The first of these goals was a classic. Here's how to practise it in the playground:

Stand in the penalty area waiting for a cross from the wing. When the ball comes over, get to it before the player marking you and trap it on your chest...

...as the ball comes down flick it over the head of another defender rushing in to tackle you...

...as the ball comes down again don't wait for it to bounce...

... but volley it into the net! (You may need to practise this a few million times before you get it right – unless your name is Pelé the Second!)

Here are some more facts about the brilliant Brazilians.

- Brazil are the only country to have played in every single World Cup finals.
- They've won the trophy five times – in 1958, 1962, 1970, 1994 and 2002.

THE UNBEATEN BEATEN AWARD...

Bolivia – when they beat Brazil in a 1994 qualifier it was the first time Brazil had ever lost a qualifying match. They'd stayed unbeaten for 60 years!

- Djalma Santos, a defender in Brazil's 1958 team, nearly didn't become a footballer. His father caught him playing truant from school and stopped him from playing football until he'd passed his exams!

- Garrincha, an amazing winger who played in the 1958 and 1962 winning teams nearly didn't become a footballer either – for a much more serious reason. As a child he'd contracted a disease which had left him with badly deformed legs. He overcame this affliction so well that in the 1962 final, when Brazil played Czechoslovakia, the man marking him stopped trying to win the ball and stood watching him with his hands on his hips!

- Even Brazilian non-players are quick on their feet! The moment the referee blew his whistle to end the 1958 final, Americo, the team's trainer, raced on and stole the ball from him as souvenir!

- Because most Brazilians have very complicated names, most are known by nicknames. Let's face it, if you were a TV commentator would you prefer to say "It's a great goal by Edson Arantes do Nascimento!" or "It's a great goal by Pelé!"?

Wicked World Cup question
The first Brazilian to receive a winners' medal was Anfilogino Guarisi, in 1934 ... a year when Brazil were knocked out in the first round. How did he do it?

Wicked answer: He was playing for Italy!

Pelé – The most brilliant Brazilian of them all

Pelé is probably the most famous footballer in the world. He won three World Cup winners' medals with Brazil and countless other honours. But, if he'd had his own way, everybody would have still been calling him by his real name: Edson Arantes do Nascimento. After the other kids at school made up the nickname for him, Pelé didn't like it and would start a fight with anybody who used it. Fortunately for everybody else, this got him into so  much trouble he decided it was better to keep his nickname and concentrate on his football.

Well, rag-ball rather than football. Born into a poor family, Pelé didn't have a football of his own until he was ten. Before that, he played barefoot in the streets with a ball made of rags!

Then, when he did get boots and a ball, his team didn't have a decent set of shirts. Pelé helped solve this problem himself. Trains used to pass near his home, their open wagons piled high with the peanut harvest (nuts of all sorts grow in Brazil). Not surprisingly, as the train rattled along a few peanuts would fall off. What did Pelé do? Picked them up and sold them until his team had enough money for the shirts they needed!

Leaving school at 14, he became an apprentice shoemaker (at least he'd learn how to make his own boots!) but didn't complete the apprenticeship. By then, his talent had already been recognized and a year later, when he was just 15, Pelé gave up shoemaking and became the youngest player in the Brazilian league with his club, Santos. Another year on, aged 16, he played his first international for Brazil!

His career with Santos was amazing. In 1,114 games, Pelé scored an incredible 1,090 goals! His 1,000th goal came from a penalty.

When the referee awarded it, nobody in the crowd was left in any doubt about what was going to happen. The stadium announcer told the crowd this was going to be Pelé's 1,000th goal – before he ran in to take the kick! Pelé was so popular in Brazil by then that his country even issued a special commemorative postage stamp to mark the feat.

His fame was worldwide. During one match for Santos in Colombia, the referee sent Pelé off by mistake – it should have been another Santos player. Pelé was back in the dressing room and unlacing his boots when he was told to go back out again. The huge crowd had been so annoyed at what had happened that they were setting fire to cushions and throwing them on the pitch! To avoid a full-scale riot it had been decided that Pelé must return and the referee must go. The referee's place was taken by one of the linesmen and Pelé completed the match!

Pelé made 91 appearances for Brazil, 14 of them in the final rounds of four different World Cup tournaments. In those games he scored 12 goals – but he's almost as famous for the goals he just missed.

During the 1970 tournament he almost scored from the half-way line against Peru. Then in the semi-final against Uruguay, he raced after a through ball and:

... let it run past one side of the Uruguayan's onrushing goalkeeper while....

... he ran round the other side of the goalkeeper then....

... caught up with the ball and, as a defender rushed back to cover....

.....Pelé hit it past him only to shave the far post instead of scoring!

Pelé retired from the game in 1974, only to be persuaded to come back a year later to play for New York Cosmos in the newly-formed North American Soccer League (NASL). After helping Cosmos win the title, he finally retired for good in 1977 – and the NASL promptly collapsed!

Pelé became Brazil's Minister for Sport in 1994. He now spends his time touring the world as an ambassador for his country – a far cry from the 17-year-old who burst into tears at the end of the 1958 final.

I hate to think how he's going to behave when we **DON'T** win!

Nutty nicknames

Like the Brazilians, some players are given nicknames because their real names are either too long, or too hard to pronounce. Others, though, have been given nicknames to describe the sort of players

they are – and some of them have been wicked!
See if you can match the players to their nicknames
in this quiz.

PLAYERS

1 GARRINCHA (BRAZIL 1958) – A speedy winger.
2 BENITO LORENZI (ITALY 1954) – Who was always arguing with the referee.
3 GEORGIO GHEZZI (ITALY 1954) – A madly diving goalkeeper.
4 LEV YASHIN (RUSSIA 1966) – A goalkeeper with long arms and an outfit that didn't show the mud.
5 SIGVARD PARLING (SWEDEN 1958) – A solid defender.
6 ALAN SHEARER (ENGLAND 1998) – A crisp striker.
7 GERD MÜLLER (WEST GERMANY 1970) – A solid attacker.
8 RYAN GIGGS (WALES, IF THEY EVER REACH THE FINALS AGAIN) – A friendly youngster.

NICKNAMES

A) POISON

B) FATTY

C) THE BLACK OCTOPUS

D) THE CORDIAL KID

Pleased to meet you.

E) LITTLE BIRD

H) SMOKY

F) KAMIKAZE

G) THE IRON STOVE

1962: BRILLIANT BRAZIL-AGAIN

Host Country
CHILE

Winners
BRAZIL

Runners Up
CZECHOSLOVAKIA

No. of Teams
Entered **56**

Third Place
CHILE

No. of Teams
in Finals **16**

Fourth Place
YUGOSLAVIA

Goals Scored
89 IN 32 GAMES

Top Scorers

DRAZEN JERKOVIC (Yugoslavia) - 4 GOALS IN 6 GAMES

FLORIAN ALBERT (Hungary) - 4 GOALS IN 3 GAMES

VALENTIN IVANOV (Russia) - 4 GOALS IN 4 GAMES

GARRINCHA (Brazil) - 4 GOALS IN 6 GAMES

VAVA (Brazil) - 4 GOALS IN 6 GAMES

LEONEL SANCHEZ (Chile) - 4 GOALS IN 6 GAMES

England were the only British team who qualified for the 1962 finals in Chile. They put up their best performance to date, reaching the quarter-finals before being beaten 1-3 by the eventual winners, Brazil.

In this game the Brazilian winger Garrincha was at his wicked best, scoring two goals and making the other. One of them was a header, for which he managed to out-jump Maurice Norman, the England defender – even though Norman was 20 cm (8 in) taller!

Little Bird! Little Kangaroo, more like!

From there, Brazil cruised to the final where they beat Czechoslovakia 3-1 to retain the title they'd won in 1958.

THE FOUL FOOTBALLS AWARD...

Chile. Unfortunately the Chilean-made footballs kept going flat or losing their shape – or both! So, to spare their feelings, referees would start the game with a Chilean football, only to swap it for a decent one the first time it went out of play!

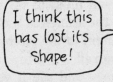

I think this has lost its shape!

Talking of footballs, the Brazilian trainer Americo doubled his collection in Chile. At the end of the final he raced on and swiped the ball from the referee just as he'd done in Sweden!

Medicine men

One non-footballing lesson that England learned in 1962 was to take their own doctor with them. They went to Chile without one, and it nearly cost an England player his life. Peter Swan, the Sheffield Wednesday defender, fell ill. He'd contracted dysentery, an illness that makes you go to the toilet a lot. This would have been bad enough, but when the local doctor looked at him he diagnosed Swan as having a different kind of stomach problem. What did he prescribe? A laxative – to make him go to the toilet!

Nowadays, teams have their own medical teams with them – from doctors behind the scenes to those with their boxes of tricks who run on to the pitch to deal with any player who gets injured.

Play this wicked medical game – and see if you survive!

THE MEDICAL GAME

1 BAD COLLISION – MISS A TURN.
In 1930 the Paraguayan player Lino Nessi broke his leg in the match against Belgium – by colliding with a goal post!

2 KNOCK YOURSELF OUT – CARRIED BACK TO THE START!
In the 1930 semi-final between Argentina and USA, the USA medical assistant was so angered by a refereeing decision he threw his medical bag on the ground, breaking a bottle of chloroform (an anaesthetic). He was carried off!

M.D.

4 KNOCKED OUT BY YOUR TEAM MATES – NO GOES FOR 10 MINUTES
In 1954 the Uruguayan Hohlberg equalised against Hungary – and was promptly knocked unconcious by his celebrating team mates! He had to go off and Hungary went on to win!

I wish I'd missed!

3 CALL A DOCTOR QUICKLY – HAVE ANOTHER TURN
When the Brazil player Nariz broke his wrist during the 1938 Tournament he had no problem getting treatment: he was a doctor himself!

Hm!

5 IGNORE A FEVER – RUN AROUND EVEN MORE.
Before the 1962 final against Czechoslovakia the Brazilian winger Garrincha had a temperature of 40°c (104°f). He played – and was 'hot stuff'!

SMASH!

6 SUFFER FROM SUNBURN IN A SENSITIVE PLACE – STAY IN THE SHADE FOR 2 TURNS
Mexico's high altitude and thin air, which made the sunlight more powerful, caused Bobby Charlton of England to suffer from sunburn in 1970 – on his bald patch!

CARRIED ON OVER

77

10 **HAVE AN INJECTION— GO BACKWARDS, FAST!**
Contracting tonsillitis in 1986 proved a double embarrassment for England's Trevor Steven. Firstly he had to have an injection in the bum. Secondly, because the regular doctor was unavailable another doctor was called— a stranger!!

SUN CREAM

FALSE ALARM— 9 DO NOTHING UNTIL THE NEXT DAY
Before travelling to Colorado Springs in preparation for the 1986 finals in Mexico, England manager Bobby Robson gave his players a severe warning about the dangers of sunbathing at high altitude. The moment they arrived it snowed for 7 hours non-stop, and they couldn't go out at all!

8 **NOTHING LEFT TO GIVE — MISS NEXT GAME— ALMOST**
In 1982 Northern Ireland's Sammy McIlroy and Sammy Nelson were selected for drugs testing after a game against Spain in boiling heat. They'd become so dehydrated they both had to spend over 2 hours in the loo, and the team almost missed their plane to the next match.

Er, can I borrow some of yours?

THE MEDICAL GAME (CONTINUED)

Tooth Hurty!

No, Mick, kick off 3 o'clock as usual.

TOOTH-ACHE NEARLY MISS A TURN
England defender Mick Mills almost missed the plane to a 1970 match against Romania. He was at the dentist

78

WATER NEEDED – GO ROUND IN CIRCLES

Again in 1986, in the heat of Spain, Chris Waddle came on as England sub carrying 6 plastic bags of water for his team mates - only for the ball to come his way immediately. Thinking quickly, he put the bags down, beat a defender, then picked the bags up again to hand around!

11

12

BAD TOE – PUT YOUR FEET UP FOR A WHILE.

England Striker Gary Lineker injured his toe so badly in 1990 that he couldn't fit his foot into his boot... ...So he trained in a pair of slippers!

HAVE AN OPERATION, LOSE YOUR SHIRT, BUT WIN THE GAME AND HELP OTHERS TO WIN AS WELL!

Tostao, a member of Brazil's 1970 winning team, was only able to play because of an eye operation performed by an American surgeon. He gave the surgeon his shirt and winners medal then, after retiring from football, went on to qualify as a doctor himself!

79

No smoking!

Finally, everybody knows that smoking is a danger to your health. Here are two wicked World Cup tales about it.

- The England squad preparing for the 1986 finals were invited to join the "No Smoking Campaign" being run by the Health Council. When manager Bobby Robson checked up, he found only one person who did smoke – the team doctor!

- FIFA didn't set a particularly good example that year, either. They not only accepted sponsorship money from the cigarette company Camel, but allowed them to float a huge yellow cigarette balloon outside Mexico's Azteca Stadium on the day of the final.

Proof, if any more were needed, that cigarettes really do damage your health

80

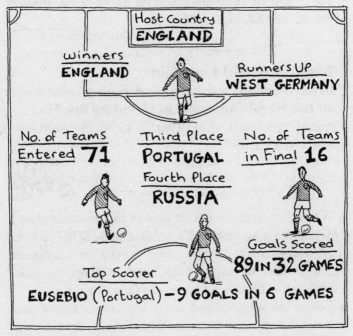

Host Country
ENGLAND

Winners
ENGLAND

Runners Up
WEST GERMANY

No. of Teams Entered **71**

Third Place
PORTUGAL

Fourth Place
RUSSIA

No. of Teams in Final **16**

Goals Scored
89 IN 32 GAMES

Top Scorer
EUSEBIO (Portugal) – 9 GOALS IN 6 GAMES

This was England's year in every way. They won the World Cup but Scotland, Northern Ireland and Wales didn't even qualify for the finals.

Here's your wicked guide to England's progress to become world champions.

Before the tournament even began

● Tickets for the World Cup final were freely available. All you had to do was buy tickets for lots of other games at the same time. Compared to today's prices, they sound ridiculously inexpensive: a ticket for the cheapest part of any ground for ten matches including the final cost just £3.87½p – that's less than 40p per game! Even the most expensive ticket, giving you a seat in the main stand for every game, worked out at only £2.55 a game!

Wicked World Cup fact
If you'd bought a souvenir programme covering all the World Cup matches including the final it would have cost you 12½p … today it could be worth over £100!

- What you couldn't get at any of the grounds was a drink in a glass bottle. To counter some of the threats of hooliganism, drinks were served in cardboard containers or paper cups, rather than in glass beakers or bottles which nasty fans could throw.
- For a while it looked as if the other thing that wouldn't be seen in a World Cup match was the trophy itself. While on display at a London stamp exhibition it was stolen. A massive police operation swung into action, only for the trophy to be found under a bush by a dog named "Pickles".

Just call me the F.A. pup!

So famous did Pickles become that he was allowed to attend the posh hotel celebration party after England's win. His owner, David Corbett, was given a reward of £3,000 – three times more than each of the England players got for winning the trophy!

- As the tournament got under way, though, it seemed that everybody in the country wanted England to win ... even the person who stole the trophy! Edward Bletchley said before attending court, "whatever my sentence is, I hope that England wins the World Cup". It didn't make the judge feel any kinder towards him. He was given two years in prison!

The opening group matches

- England's first game, and the opening game of the finals, was a terrible 0-0 draw against Uruguay. This result seemed to start a wicked trend. The opening game of the World Cup finals didn't see a goal for the next 16 years either! The three tournaments which followed all  began with 0-0 draws until Belgium broke the run by scoring against Argentina in 1982.

- England's second match against Mexico looked as if it was going the same way until the desperate Wembley crowd began to chant, "We want goals! We want goals!" Almost at once, England's Bobby Charlton raced from the half-way line to bang in a rocket shot! England went on to win 2-0.

- The final group match against France was also a 2-0 win for England. It was in this match that England's tough-tackling midfielder, Nobby Stiles, was booked for a foul ... but not by the referee! A FIFA official was sitting in the stand and he issued the caution after the match was over.

The quarter-final: England v Argentina

- It was in this game, which England won 1-0, that Argentina's captain, Antonio Rattin, was sent off for arguing with the referee. What made this so different was that Rattin was arguing in Spanish but the referee spoke only his native German! But understanding what Rattin had said wasn't important. As the referee explained afterwards, "I sent him off because of the look on his face"!

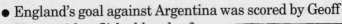

- England's goal against Argentina was scored by Geoff Hurst with a flicked header from a curling cross by his West Ham teammate Martin Peters. They'd practised this move dozens of times at West Ham's training ground – except that, instead of real defenders, they'd used wooden posts set in concrete-filled buckets!

Semi-final: England v Portugal

- England won this terrific match 2-1, with both goals being scored by Bobby Charlton. The second was such a cracker, a low shot that whistled into the corner of the net, that a number of the Portuguese players shook his hand as he ran back to the centre circle.

THE TOLD-YOU-SO AWARD...

Every England player except goalkeeper Gordon Banks. Portugal's goal in the semi-final was a penalty, scored by their star striker Eusebio. Banks knew that Eusebio always put his kicks to the goalkeeper's right. So did his teammates, who all pointed that way. Thinking that Eusebio would see all this and change his mind, Banks dived to his left. Eusebio put it to his right, as usual!

World Cup final: England v Germany

● A famous match. England were 2-1 up with seconds to go when Germany equalized. In extra time Geoff Hurst hit the bar and the linesman insisted that the ball crossed the line as it crashed down. Then, in the very last minute, Hurst staggered through and whacked in a great shot to complete his hat trick and give England a 4-2 victory. It's a brilliant goal ... isn't it?

Wicked World Cup quote

"All I wanted to do was hit it as hard as I possibly could, with every ounce of my strength, thinking, 'if it goes over, then fine'. I knew it was only seconds before the end, it's 50 yards behind the goal at Wembley, and if I hit it into the car park it'll take that few seconds and the game will be over." **Geoff Hurst**

- While all this drama was going on, the organizers were taking no chances about having the trophy stolen again! It was in a Wembley office throughout the match, being guarded by two detectives and a secretary named Sally Ellis. They had to watch the match on TV. When it ended, the three of them had just enough time for a quick cheer before the detectives took the cup up to be presented by the Queen.

After the match

- England defender Jack Charlton was given a trophy of his very own. During the tournament he'd been drawn out of the hat three times to take a random drugs test and he was picked yet again after the final. In recognition, the testers

87

handed him a baby's potty inscribed: *presented to J Charlton, who gave his best for his country.*

 ## MOST MISERABLE FOOTBALLER IN THE WORLD AWARD...

Denis Law, of Scotland – who was such a non-fan of the English team that he went out to play a round of golf rather than watch the World Cup final on TV. On returning to the clubhouse the cheering members told him that England had won. "It was the blackest day of my life," he said – and he meant it.

Serious superstitions

Fancy yourself as a World Cup winner, like the England midfielder Nobby Stiles? A superstitious man, he took no chances. If you want to be like him, here's what you've got to do before the match even starts!

- Wear the same shirt as you wore for the last game that England didn't lose ...
- and the same pair of cufflinks, the same tie, the same shoes, the same socks and ...
- the same underpants! (You can wash them in between games.)

Then it's time to get changed:

- put on your shorts and shirt ...
- coat the inside of your boots with grease ...
- soak your feet in hot water ...
- then put on your socks and boots ...
- before taking your shirt off again and rubbing olive oil into your chest ...
- and your legs ...

- before replacing your shirt ...
- then knotting your tie-ups ...
- and greasing your face and hands.
  Finally, you go to a mirror and ...
- take off your glasses and put in your contact lenses ...
- take out your false front teeth, and ...
- comb your hair.

Then, if you're not too exhausted, you go out and play brilliantly!

Nobby Stiles wasn't the only England player to have superstitions...

- Whenever England stayed in a hotel, Bobby Charlton and left-back Ray Wilson were room-mates. They always packed and unpacked their bags in the same fixed order: first this boot, then that one, then this shin pad...

89

- Jack Charlton had a clutch of superstitions. He would change his studs at the last minute, always go on to the pitch last, and when on the pitch he would have to score during the warm up. This last ritual gave him trouble in the World Cup final because he missed the goal with his first shot! He had to grab another ball quickly so that he could bang it in!

Footballers seem to be a superstitious bunch anyway...

- Carlos Bilardo, the winning Argentine coach in 1986, certainly was. He had borrowed some toothpaste from one of his players before the first match and so did the same thing all the way through the competition. He also made his players come out and line up for the national anthem in the same order every time.

- England's Alan Shearer believed in an unusual good luck mascot – his mother-in-law! She watched him score on his England début, but didn't see the next four games when he failed to score. When she came again, he started scoring once more!

90

1970: BRAZIL GO NUTS

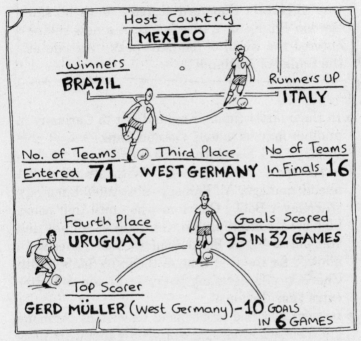

Host Country
MEXICO

Winners
BRAZIL

Runners UP
ITALY

No. of Teams Entered **71**

Third Place
WEST GERMANY

No of Teams In Finals **16**

Fourth Place
URUGUAY

Goals Scored
95 IN 32 GAMES

Top Scorer
GERD MÜLLER (West Germany)—**10** GOALS IN **6** GAMES

Northern Ireland, Scotland and Wales failed to qualify for the 1970 finals. England managed it – but they had a pretty simple task. As reigning champions they qualified automatically!

England managed to reach the quarter-finals, even though they were drawn in the same opening group as the eventual winners, Brazil. When the two teams played each other, Brazil won 1-0. The match is famous for England goalkeeper Gordon Banks's save of a shot from Pelé. Sprawling on his goal-line to reach a header from the Brazilian player, Banks managed to flick it over the bar!

- In the quarter-finals, England lost to Germany in another famous match. Gordon Banks wasn't able to play, and his place was taken by the Chelsea goalkeeper, Peter Bonetti. With England 2-1 ahead, manager Alf Ramsey substituted England's star player Bobby Charlton who, until that point, had been cancelling out Germany's captain and star player Franz Beckenbauer. (Substitutes were allowed for the first time in the 1970 finals.) With Charlton off, Germany went on to win 3-2 after extra time. Boo-hoo!

- Beckenbauer had problems of his own as Germany lost their semi-final against Italy 3-4 after extra time. He'd injured his arm late in the second half. By then, though, Germany had used their two substitutes so Beckenbauer had to play through extra time with his arm in a sling. Talk about a hand-icap!

- Italy went on to meet Brazil in the final. Both countries were aiming for their third World Cup win, which would mean being given the Jules Rimet trophy to keep for ever. Brazil won the match 4-1, took the solid gold figurine home, and kept it...

- No, not for ever. Only until 1984, when it was stolen and melted down. The famous trophy no longer exists.

THE 'IF AT FIRST YOU DON'T SUCCEED' AWARD...

Belgium. They won their first ever World Cup finals game in 1970 – 40 years after taking part in the opening tournament in 1930!

Wicked wonders: the two Bobbys of England

Some great players have appeared in the World Cup for England over the years. Two of the greatest shared the same first name: Bobby Charlton and Bobby Moore.

Bobby Charlton was born in Ashington, in the North East of England, and learned to play the game in the back streets of his home town. He was picked to play for East Northumberland Schools. It was during a schools match that he was spotted by a Manchester United scout who reported back to the United manager, Matt Busby: "This boy could be a world-beater!"

Bobby Moore got a slightly different report. Born in the East End of London, he played for Barking and Leyton Schools. It was a West Ham scout who spotted him as a 15 year old. His report said, "This boy certainly impressed me with his tenacity and industry." It also went on to predict, "He may not set the world alight."

The United scout was right, the West Ham scout wrong. Both players went on to become instantly recognizable world stars – Charlton with his swerve, bullet shot and bald head, Moore with his blond hair, calm defending and immaculate appearance. (When playing for West Ham he often had creases ironed down the front of his shorts, as though they were a pair of trousers!)

Bobby Charlton played for Manchester United throughout his whole career, breaking into the side when he was 19. Only fate saved him from ending his career just two years later. Returning from a European Cup match, the aeroplane carrying the team crashed when trying to take off from Munich airport. Twenty-three people died, including eight United players, but Bobby Charlton walked away with hardly a scratch. From then on he became a central figure in United's team, winning every honour in the game.

Bobby Moore went on to become West Ham's youngest captain, then, at the age of 23, captain of the England team. Moore was a terrific defender, and Pelé rated him the toughest opponent he'd ever faced. He didn't score many goals but, when he did, how did he react? He just turned round and ran back to the centre-circle for the kick-off, leaving his teammates to get on with the hugging and kissing.

Bobby Charlton's reaction was rather different. Whenever one of his rocket shots hit the back of the net he'd leap in the air and shout, "She's there!" He scored 249 goals for Manchester United in 758 League, Cup and European Cup appearances.

One of the goals *wasn't* against Leeds United, the team his brother Jack played for. Jack was a tough defender and the boys' mother, Cissie, would often warn Jack not to kick Bobby when the two teams were playing each other. On one occasion, though, Bobby's wizardry left Jack sitting on his backside. As he leapt up and raced after his brother, Jack was heard to yell at him: "Don't even think about scoring!"

The 1970 finals were the last the two players appeared in. After becoming the only England captain to lift the World Cup (so far!) in 1966, Bobby Moore almost missed the 1970 tournament altogether. Before a warm-up match in Colombia on the way to Mexico, he'd been falsely accused of stealing a bracelet from a jeweller's shop in Bogota and arrested. He was released after two days to join the rest of the team. A later investigation discovered similar cases involving other celebrities who'd visited Colombia – ranging from singers to bullfighters! Eventually, two years later, the guilty parties were charged with conspiracy. Maybe the police should have listened to the England squad member who pointed out that their captain didn't need to steal. "Steal a bracelet? If Bobby had wanted he could have bought the whole shop!"

Bobby Moore finally ended his international career with a grand total of 108 international caps. Bobby Charlton retired after the 1970 tournament. He'd won 106 England caps. His 49 England goals are second only to Wayne Rooney's 50.

The 100 club

Charlton and Moore may have cracked the 100-cap barrier for playing for their country, but they weren't the first – and neither of them hold the record for numbers of caps.

Billy Wright was the first England player to win 100 caps, eventually going on to win 105. He was England's captain, and played in the 1950 and 1954 tournaments. Amazingly for a defender, he was never booked – either for his club (Wolverhampton Wanderers) or his country!

Peter Shilton is the most-capped England player of all time with 125 caps. He played in three World Cups for England, in 1982, 1986 and 1990. He also played over 1,000 league games in his career.

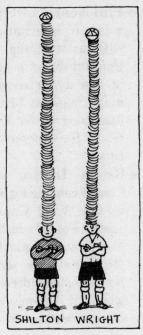

SHILTON   WRIGHT

David Beckham, **Ashley Cole**, **Steven Gerrard**, **Frank Lampard** and **Wayne Rooney** are recent members of the '100' club. In celebration, each received a special gold 100th cap in a glass case.

The not-so-greats

No footballer is picked for their country unless they are a pretty terrific player – but some who were selected for England didn't always make the biggest impact...

- **Viv Anderson** of Nottingham Forest, was in the squads for both the 1982 and 1986 finals but didn't play in a single game.

- **Phil Neal** of Liverpool once won an international cap without touching the ball. Coming on as a substitute in the dying seconds of a match against France, he'd just lined up for a free kick when the referee blew for time!

- **Kevin Hector** of Derby County came on for 90 seconds in the World Cup qualifier against Poland which England had to win to qualify for the 1974 finals. He scraped the post, England drew 1-1 and went out. He only made one more appearance for England.

1974 · GERMAN GENIUS

Host Country
WEST GERMANY

Winners
WEST GERMANY

Runners Up
NETHERLANDS

No. of Teams Entered **98**

Third Place
POLAND

No of Teams in Finals **16**

Fourth Place
BRAZIL

Goals Scored **97** IN **38** GAMES

Top Scorer
GRZEGORZ LATO (Poland) – **7** GOALS IN **7** GAMES

Scotland were the only British country to qualify for the 1974 finals. They had a curious first round.
Record: only country out of the 16 finalists to stay unbeaten;
Result: knocked out!
Yes, although winning one game and drawing two, they came third in their group on goal difference!

Favourites to win the tournament were the stylish Dutch, led by their captain Johan Cruyff. He had a favourite trick for beating a defender who was marking him. Try it. The trick goes like this:

With the ball between your feet, turn sideways so that your left arm is facing the defender....

...guide the ball away from the defender with your left foot then (and this is the hard bit!)....

...flick it with the inside of your right foot so that it goes between your legs and past the defender...

....spin round and race after it while the defender's wondering where the ball's gone.

Wicked World Cup fact
The start of the 1974 final was delayed ... because nobody had remembered to put out the corner posts!

Netherlands reached the final in 1974, where they met West Germany. It was a match with the most sensational start in World Cup history. Netherlands kicked off, exchanging 16 passes until Cruyff got the ball. He sprinted into the German penalty area ... and was fouled. Netherlands scored from the penalty to go 1-0 up inside a minute! It didn't last, though. The Germans came back to win 2-1.

England were represented in this final. How? The referee who gave the first-minute penalty, Jack Taylor, came from England.

THE FIRST HOLDER OF THE WORLD CUP (AGAIN) AWARD...

Silvio Gazzaniga, the Italian sculptor who won the international competition to design the successor to the Jules Rimet trophy for use in 1974. Called "The FIFA World Cup", it is 36 cm high, made of 6 kgs of 18 carat gold and shows two human figures holding up the globe. The trophy has been designed to last until 2038. After that there'll be no more room on the base to engrave the names of the winners!

Wicked wonders: 'Kaiser Franz' and Germany

Germany's overall record in the World Cup is one of non-stop success. Here are the wicked facts about it.

- Germany have won the trophy four times (1954, 1974, 1990, 2014), been losing finalists four times (1966, 1982, 1986 and 2002) and semi-finalists five times (1934, 1958, 1970, 2006 and 2010).
- Not bad for a country which didn't have full-time professional footballers until 1963!
- They've qualified for the final tournament every time they've entered. They didn't enter in 1930, and weren't allowed to enter in 1950 because

FIFA had expelled them in 1946 following the Second World War. Who knows, they might have won both those competitions too!

- Between the 1950 and 1990 there were actually two German teams – East Germany and West Germany. The country had been divided after the war. The successful team was West Germany – and they did it using only half the players in their country!

- East Germany's record in the World Cup is pretty hopeless. Their magic moment, though, came in 1974 when they reached the final tournament and were put in the same group as West Germany. They beat the eventual winners 1-0!

- Nowadays, with Germany united again, there's just one team: Germany. It was a full German side that competed in 1994. They only reached the quarter-finals, their worst performance for 16 years!

Wicked World Cup fact
The German striker, Gerd Müller, scored 68 goals in 62 matches. Most strikers build up their tally by scoring in friendlies. Not Müller. Almost all of these goals were in European Championship or World Cup games.

Franz Beckenbauer

From trainee insurance salesman to "Emperor" of Germany – that's the story of Franz Beckenbauer, Germany's captain in 1974. Out of all the top World Cup stars, Franz Beckenbauer is unique. He's the only one who's been successful as both a player and a coach.

Aged 17, he started his full-time playing career with the German club Bayern Munich after giving up his job with an insurance company. He made his début for them at the age of 19 – on the left wing. But it *wasn't* as a winger that Franz Beckenbauer was to become so famous that the German fans would nickname him the "Kaiser" (the Emperor). The position which he made his own was that of attacking sweeper.

Not many players can claim to have invented a whole new style of play, but Franz Beckenbauer did. Until he came along, central defenders usually chose one of two options when they won the ball:

– they kicked it into the stands

– they kicked it over the stands!

Beckenbauer showed that a defender who could spring into attack could be as big a match-winner as any forward. He scored many goals, a typical example being one against Switzerland in 1966. Try this one the next time you have a big match in your street:

Break from defence. Pass to your striker, but keep on running...

...get the return ball as you run into the other team's penalty area....

...with your right foot push it between two defenders as they dive in to tackle you....

...then, with your left foot, slip it past the goalkeeper into the net!

Franz Beckenbauer could also whack them in from a distance. Ask England – he scored one against them in 1970.

Becoming captain of both his club side and his country, Beckenbauer went on to finish his international career with 103 caps.

What then? After eight years away, some of them playing in America, he returned to become Germany's coach – and the success began again!

Under his guidance, Germany went on to appear in two more World Cup finals. They lost in 1986 but when they triumphed in 1990, Beckenbauer became the first man to have been a winner both as a player and a coach.

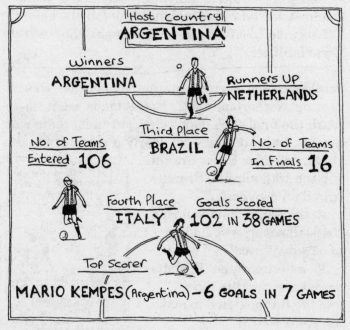

Host Country
ARGENTINA

Winners
ARGENTINA

Runners Up
NETHERLANDS

Third Place
BRAZIL

No. of Teams Entered **106**

No. of Teams In Finals **16**

Fourth Place
ITALY

Goals Scored
102 IN **38** GAMES

Top Scorer

MARIO KEMPES (Argentina) – **6** GOALS IN **7** GAMES

1978 saw the same story as 1974 as far as the British teams were concerned. Only Scotland qualified to go to Argentina, and they were knocked out in the first round – again.

In fact, the Scots team didn't have a happy time of it at all. Even their training didn't go well. One player moaned: "the training pitch takes an hour to get to, and it's so bad the cows won't eat the grass on it!"

Worse was to come. After Scotland's first match, which they lost 1-3 to Peru, their winger Willie Johnston failed a drugs test. He admitted taking pep pills and was sent home.

Scotland's one success in the competition was in beating Netherlands 3-2. Netherlands went on to reach the final. The match that put them there was against Italy. It was very nearly a disaster for the Dutch defender Ernie Brandts...

– in the 18th minute, Brandts scored an own goal...

– at the same time injuring his goalkeeper, who had to be substituted!

– 30 minutes later, Brandts scored again – this time into the Italians' goal to make the score 1-1.

– Netherlands went on to win the game 2-1.

Argentina reached the final in a controversial way. In 1978 the second round was played in league groups, not as a knockout, with the top teams in each group going into the final. Argentina went into their last group match needing to beat fellow South American country Peru by at least 4-0; if they didn't, Brazil would go into the final. What happened? Argentina, amazingly, won 6-0! Afterwards it was claimed that the Argentine government had bribed the Peru players to lose. In retaliation, some Argentine newspapers claimed that it had been Brazil who'd been offering bribes to Peru – to play well!

The final that nearly didn't happen

Argentina may not have been guilty of bribery, but they definitely tried some wicked tactics at the start of the final...

● The team stayed behind in the changing rooms for several minutes, leaving Holland to be jeered at by the massive crowd.

● Then, just as the match was about to kick off, they complained that a plaster cast being worn by Holland's Rene Van de Kerkhof was dangerous and that he shouldn't be allowed to play (even though he'd been wearing it for ages). The issue was only sorted out when the Dutch players threatened to go off and leave the Argentinians to play the final on their own! Maybe they should have. Argentina went on to win the game 3-1.

The terrible telly

The 1930 World Cup competition was watched by 434,500 spectators – and zero TV viewers! Television coverage wasn't available. Nowadays, of course, television audiences are massive. The 2014 tournament in Brazil was beamed into every country on planet Earth, with at least one billion people watching the final itself! But is it always a good thing to have the World Cup matches on TV? Try your hand at this wicked TV quiz to find out!

1 In 1994, Russian policemen were happy for the matches to be on TV. Why?
2 In 1978, Italy played England in an afternoon qualifying match but neither the Italian nor the English TV companies dared show the game live. Why not?
3 During the 1986 finals in Mexico, the players would have been happier if the games hadn't been on TV. Why?
4 In 1994 a security guard in Thailand wished he'd left his TV turned off instead of watching a match. Why?

5 A Frenchman wanted to watch a game on TV in 1982, but his wife wanted to talk. What went off?

6 Referees didn't have a lot of time for TV in 1986. Why not?

7 The citizens of Bangladesh wanted their TVs on in 1990, but they weren't. What did they do instead?

8 In Khartoum the electricity companies flashed a message across TV screens telling viewers there'd be power cuts unless they could reduce the demand for electricity in some other way. What happened?

9 Two people in Germany were glad the TV was on for Germany's match against Bulgaria in 1994, even though they didn't want to watch. Why not?

10 Finally, in 2010, the government of North Korea was happy for TVs to be on, but only if one team was playing. Which team?

Answers:

1 The crime rate dropped by 70% as crooks stayed in to watch the matches!

2 They thought too many people would take time off work to watch.

3 The time of day when the TV companies said they'd get the biggest worldwide audiences just happened to be the hottest time of the day in Mexico. It was a case of the players overheating instead of the TVs!

4 While he watched, bank robbers carried out a safe filled with money!

5 What went off was a gun. The woman got so annoyed at her husband for not answering her questions that she shot him. Talk about a deadly shot!

6 The "time" was the extra added on for stoppages. It was claimed that FIFA told them to keep it down to save the TV companies money on satellite bookings!

7 They had a riot. The TVs weren't on because of a power breakdown, so everybody went out and attacked the power station instead.

8 The whole city was immediately plunged into darkness as everybody turned off everything except their TVs!

9 They were prisoners, and they were too busy escaping from their cell using bed sheets while their warders watched the match.

10 North Korea. The country's leader, Kim Jong-il, only let their games be shown – always edited to make North Korea look the better team! They must have been short programmes. North Korea lost every game, including a 0-7 defeat by Portugal!

Wicked words

Wherever the TV cameras are, not far away you'll find a panel of crazy commentators and pitiful pundits to tell the viewers what they think. At least, that's the way it's been since 1970. That was the year when the first ever World Cup panel was used by ITV.

The panel started off with three members: Pat Crerand, formerly of Manchester United and Scotland; Malcolm Allison, coach at Manchester City; and Derek Dougan, formerly of Wolverhampton Wanderers and Northern Ireland.

When England were knocked out, the panel were joined by a member of the England squad who'd flown back from Mexico – Arsenal's Bob McNab. By then, though, the other three had got used to talking a lot. Poor McNab couldn't get a word in. The TV producer solved the problem by giving him a little flag to wave. When McNab flapped it, the other three panel members had to shut up!

Here are some wicked words from people who might wish they hadn't opened their mouths:
● As one player shaped up to take a free kick during

a game in the 1994 tournament, BBC pundit Trevor Brooking said:

• During the same tournament, Brooking's fellow BBC commentator John Motson pointed out before one match that:

• Commentators can get very excited. When Norway beat England in a 1982 qualifying match, the Norwegian commentator went completely bonkers, yelling at the top of his voice:

• No player is above criticism, even if they are Brazilian. In 1982, one critic didn't think much of the player Serginho's ball control:

When Serginho was later substituted the same critic said happily,

• At least that critic knew who he was grumbling about. Some commentators can't always manage that. Scottish commentators Bob Crampsey and Iain Archer were covering a match between Scotland and Bulgaria when Crampsey realized that he didn't know who one of the Bulgarian players was...

THE BLACK EYE AWARD...

Trevor Brooking, BBC. Before the 1996 qualifying match between England and Georgia, the two countries' media teams had a "friendly" match of their own. During the game ex-England star Trevor Brooking was badly fouled, then punched in the eye when he complained! He had to have his eyebrow stitched up before he could commentate on the real England against Georgia match!

● In 1994, when asked whether Brazilian players Romario and Bebeto would have been good enough to get into the famous team in which he played, Carlos Alberto, captain of Brazil in 1970 said:

● Again in 1994, when World Cup débutantes Saudi Arabia pulled off a surprise win against Morocco, their midfielder Fuad Amin crowed,

– forgetting that Morocco is also an Arab country!

Naughty newspapers

When it comes to wicked words, though, you can't beat a newspaper!

● One newspaper nicknamed ex-England manager Graham Taylor "turnip". After England lost a European Championship international to Sweden the headline was "Swedes 2 Turnips 1"!

● Sir Alf Ramsey, manager of England's triumphant 1966 team, wrote in a newspaper that Glen Hoddle, Peter Reid, Ray Wilkins and John Barnes were not good enough to be picked for a 1992 World Cup qualifying match. A few days later he listed his preferred squad in a different newspaper. He chose Hoddle, Reid, Wilkins and Barnes!

● Kamal al-Ganzuri, Prime Minister of Egypt, tried to have the Egyptian team removed from the newspapers. So angry was he after their 1997 qualifying round defeat by Ghana that he asked press not to mention the team for the remainder of their qualifying ties. His plan failed in a spectacular fashion. The country's biggest newspapers splashed the row across their front pages instead!

Wicked World Cup quote
Not all players talk to the media. Macedonian international Mile Hristovski wanted to find an English team, so he sent a letter directly to some clubs, describing his abilities. It began: "I was one of the greatest talents in football. Opposing players absolutely had not any chances..." and ended, "I would like to emphasize that I am a very modest man, not boastful." Needless to say, it made the newspapers!

1982: ITALIAN INSPIRATION

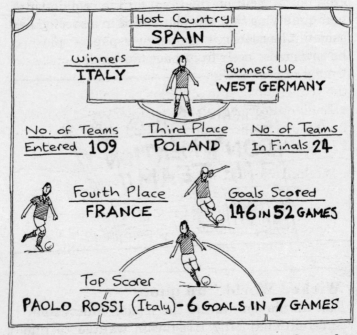

Host Country
SPAIN

Winners
ITALY

Runners Up
WEST GERMANY

No. of Teams
Entered **109**

Third Place
POLAND

No. of Teams
In Finals **24**

Fourth Place
FRANCE

Goals Scored
146 IN **52** GAMES

Top Scorer
PAOLO ROSSI (Italy) - **6** GOALS IN **7** GAMES

Things went wrong for this tournament from the very beginning – at the draw ceremony to decide which teams would be in which groups! The idea was that little footballs containing the names of the countries would be pulled out of drums. Unfortunately the wrong balls were put into the wrong drums; then when the first countries were pulled out they were put in the wrong groups; finally one ball broke, preventing any more balls being drawn until it was prised out!

Once the football got under way, England, Scotland and Northern Ireland managed to qualify for the finals. Once in Spain, Scotland managed to do their usual trick and fail to get through the first-round groups. England and Northern Ireland did a little better, getting as far as the second round. Both did something notable, though.

● Northern Ireland made history by picking Manchester United's Norman Whiteside – at 17 years 41 days, still the youngest player in a World Cup finals.

● England scored one of the quickest-ever goals in a final tournament, skipper Bryan Robson taking just 27 seconds to score against France.

Wicked World Cup quote
When short England winger Steve Coppell tried to tackle the giant German defender Hans-Peter Briegel in their 1982 second-round match, Briegel simply sniffed, "Get away, little fly."

The tournament wasn't terribly entertaining – especially the first-round match between Germany and Austria. Before the start the teams knew that a 1-0 win for Germany would allow both of them to go through to the next round of the competition. So when Germany went ahead after ten minutes, that was that. Both teams spent the remaining 80 minutes drifting about the pitch and not attempting to score. The French manager Michel Hidalgo, who'd gone to the game to spy on the two teams, suggested that they should be awarded the Nobel Peace Prize!

Hidalgo's team themselves had an eventful time. In a first-round match against Kuwait their opponents had threatened to walk off after a whistle from the crowd had stopped them playing and France had scored. Only the intervention of a member of the Kuwaiti royal family, in the shape of Prince Fahid, had persuaded them to continue – well, that and the referee changing his mind and disallowing the goal!

Then, when France met Germany in the semi-final, another wicked incident took place. Harald Schumacher, the German goalkeeper, flattened the French player Patrick Battiston with a forearm smash as the Frenchman raced towards his goal. Battiston lost two teeth and ended up in hospital, whilst Schumacher wasn't even sent off. What's more, when the match went to a penalty shoot-out (the first game in the finals ever to be decided this way) Schumacher saved two penalties to send his team into the final.

There, Germany lost 1-3 to Italy and another wicked player. The clinching goal for Italy was scored by Paulo Rossi. He'd only recently come back after a two-year ban for match-fixing (which he'd always denied).

Wicked celebrations!
Footballers like to celebrate – when they score a goal, when they win a match or, in the case of some teams, for any reason at all...

- Although the Northern Ireland squad didn't win anything, they thoroughly enjoyed themselves. Writing in his autobiography, goalkeeper Pat Jennings said that their players invariably returned from drugs testing in a merry mood. They'd all sweated so much in the Spanish heat that they'd had to tell the officials they couldn't go to the loo. Hearing this, the officials had been forced to give them bottles of beer and lager to help out! At least, the Irish players had *said* they couldn't go…

- England's celebrations had been a bit quieter, even when they scored a goal. The chairman of the FA, Sir Harold Thompson, had written a newspaper article in which he criticized players for kissing each other!

- He'd have been in trouble with the Hungarian team. In a first-round match in 1982 they beat El Salvador 10-1, the first time a team had reached double figures in a match in the finals. Three of the goals were scored in the space of ten minutes by Hungary's substitute. His name? Laszlo Kiss!

Host Country
MEXICO

Winners
ARGENTINA

Runners Up
WEST GERMANY

No. of Teams Entered **121**

Third Place
FRANCE

No. of Teams In Finals **24**

Fourth Place
BELGIUM

Goals Scored
132 IN 52 GAMES

Top Scorer

GARY LINEKER (England) – **6 GOALS IN 5 GAMES**

England, Scotland and Northern Ireland qualified for the 1986 finals, but only England made it past the first-round groups.

Northern Ireland, after starting brilliantly with a goal after just six minutes of their first match, managed only a draw and two defeats.

Scotland's performance was the same: one draw and two defeats. Once again, they'd performed poorly. Even their draw, 0-0 against Uruguay, wasn't a good result – they'd only had to play against ten men because a Uruguayan defender had been sent off in the first minute!

England reached the quarter-finals – thanks to striker Gary Lineker. Nowadays best known as Match of the Day presenter and crisps advertiser, Lineker hit a hat-trick against Poland to help England win through from their group. Another couple of Lineker goals then helped knock out Paraguay. Next up: a match against old enemies Argentina …

THE CATASTROPHIC CAPTAIN AWARD...

Ray Wilkins, England – who took over the captaincy when Bryan Robson was taken off with a dislocated collar-bone against Morocco. He lasted less than ten minutes before being sent off for throwing the ball at the referee!

Argy-bargy!
England lost against Argentina, 1-2, both of the goals being scored by the Argentinian star forward Diego Maradona. It was his first goal that caused all the controversy. This is what happened:

Amazingly neither the referee nor the linesman saw anything wrong and the goal was allowed! Two minutes later Maradona scored again, racing past four England defenders in a run from the half-way line before waltzing round Shilton to pop the ball into the net.

THE TERRIBLE CHEAT'S EXCUSE AWARD...

Diego Maradona. Asked about his punched goal after the match, Maradona claimed that it had been scored, 'a little with the head of Maradona and a little with the hand of God'.

With Maradona playing brilliantly, Argentina went on to become champions for the second time, beating Germany 3-2 in the final.

Let us in!
Perhaps England would have preferred the match to

122

be played a day earlier – then they wouldn't have been let in!

When the team turned up at the Aztec Stadium expecting to hold a training session they found the changing rooms locked. They couldn't go out to test the pitch either because it was being marked out and the grass cut. They had to go to another stadium – and only managed to get into that one thanks to their police escort calling in somebody to pick the lock on the gate!

Not that England were the first country to have stadium problems...

Non, non!
France actually withdrew from the 1950 finals in Brazil after hearing that they'd be required to play their first match in one stadium and their next game at a different stadium – 2,000 miles away!

Hang on, nearly finished!
Uruguay, host country for the first ever World Cup competition in 1930, insisted on playing their opening game in their new stadium – which wasn't yet finished. They played their first match five days after everybody else!

Feeling blue

The massive Maracana stadium in Brazil – which still holds the record for a World Cup final attendance at 199,850 – was designed with special anti-hooligan measures. The seats were painted blue, because this colour was thought to have a calming influence on people!

Wicked wonders: Diego Maradona and Argentina

Argentina's record in the World Cup has been outstanding in recent years. After losing the 1930 final to Uruguay, they did very little for the next 40 years. Then, suddenly, the team sprang to life to become champions in 1978 and 1986, and runners-up in 1990 and 2014.

The one thing that has been consistent about them, though, is controversy.

● They withdrew from the 1938 finals in retaliation against FIFA for choosing France as hosts instead of them.

● They withdrew from the 1950 finals in Brazil, this time after an argument with the Brazilian FA.

● In 1958 they were walloped 1-6 by Czechoslovakia and pelted with rubbish by their fans when they got home.

● In 1966, even before their infamous game with England, they'd had their defender, Albrecht, sent off for a rugby tackle in their first-round game with Germany.

● Then, as defending champions in 1982, they reached the second round only to be knocked out after two dreadful matches. In the first they lost

1-2 to Italy, the Italians having two players booked for kicking lumps out of the Argentine's star player and Argentina themselves doing even worse by having three players booked and one sent off. They then lost to Brazil, 1-3, this time with their star player being sent off himself.

And who was this star player? None other than that "handiest" of performers, Diego Maradona.

Wicked World Cup quote
"With Maradona, even Arsenal would have won the World Cup" – England's manager, Bobby Robson.

Maradona

Very few players in the world can have had a more amazing, up-and-down career than Diego Armando Maradona.

Born in Buenos Aires in 1960, Maradona became famous throughout Argentina as a nine-year-old ball-juggler! His brilliant ability at doing tricks with a football gave him a regular spot on a TV programme and he was seen nationwide.

Although he'd been playing matches with a junior team, Maradona then got together with some friends to form a team of their own. They called themselves "The Little Onions" – probably because they always left their opponents in tears! They must have been good because the whole team were promptly signed up by the professional club, Argentinos Juniors.

Although part of a group, Maradona was the star. Leaving school at the age of 13, he became an Argentinos Juniors player and made his debut with them at the age of 15. Just a year later, aged 16, he played his first international!

Then came the first of his set-backs. Unexpectedly, the Argentine manager dropped him from his squad just before the 1978 finals. Maradona didn't speak to him for months afterwards. Plenty of people in the country continued to criticize the decision as well, even though Argentina had become world champions.

His career recovered quickly. He was in the winning team when Argentina won the World Youth Cup and then, still a teenager, he moved to the Boca Juniors for £1 million.

Then it was time for a down-turn. Maradona had a bad 1982 World Cup, being kicked at every turn and sent off in the final game. Immediately after the tournament he came back up again, though, moving to Barcelona of Spain for a then-record fee of £3 million.

Maradona was about to enter the best spell of his career. In 1984 he left Barcelona for the Italian club Napoli for another world record fee of £5 million. Within two weeks, the club had got their money back, with interest – a flood of fans had bought 70,000 season tickets! In his seven seasons with Napoli, Maradona helped them to two Italian league titles and a UEFA Cup victory.

Then came the 1986 World Cup victory with Argentina, in which he was voted Player of the Tournament.

His "Hand of God" goal against England dented Maradona's reputation, but his second goal showed what a wonderful player he was:

Picking up the ball in his own half he took it between two England players....

...faced into the England half and cut inside a third England player...

...dribbled up to the England penalty area and past a fourth England player...

...then round the England goalkeeper...

...and stuck the ball into the net!
All with his favourite left foot!

From then on, it seemed, Maradona's career became a lot more down than up.

● He captained his side to the 1990 World Cup final, but Argentina lost and had two players sent off.

● Then, in 1991, he was arrested for taking drugs and banned from football for 15 months.

● A comeback in Spain wasn't successful, so he returned to Argentina. There he became captain again – only to fail a drugs test in the 1994 finals and be sent home in disgrace.

Another ban followed. Maradona's glorious but controversial international career was over. The former "little onion" had run onion rings around the opposition for the last time.

Wicked referees

The referee who missed Maradona's infamous "hand of God" goal was Ali Bennaceur, from Tunisia. England against Argentina had been his first game as World Cup referee. It also proved to be his last. For some reason he was never given another match to referee!

Wicked World Cup question
Who is the only referee in the history of the World Cup who could honestly claim that he was perfect?
Wicked answer: The referee from Scotland in the 1954 finals whose name really was ... Edward C *Faultless*!

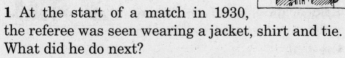

It's easy to blame the poor old referee, of course, but could you do better? Try this wicked "what happened next" quiz.

1 At the start of a match in 1930, the referee was seen wearing a jacket, shirt and tie. What did he do next?
a) Ask the way to the changing rooms.
b) Look for somebody in the crowd to be a linesman.
c) Blow his whistle to start the game.

2 In the 1930 match between France and Argentina, the referee blew for time six minutes early with France attacking dangerously. What happened next?

a) The match was declared over.
b) The teams came back to play the six minutes they'd missed.
c) France were awarded a goal.

3 In the 2006 match between Croatia and Australia, referee Graham Poll showed eight yellow cards and three reds. Croatia's Josip Simunic was a special case. What did he get?

a) Two yellows and one red.
b) One red.
c) Three yellows and one red.

4 In the 1970 match between El Salvador and Mexico, El Salvador protested against a Mexican goal by refusing to kick off again. What did the referee do?

a) Send off the El Salvador captain.
b) Blow his whistle for half-time.
c) Change his mind and disallow the goal.

5 In 1970, Welsh referee Clive Thomas was in charge of the match between Sweden and Brazil. He looked at his watch, saw that the 90 minutes were up and blew his whistle. What happened next?

a) Play carried on.
b) Brazil scored.
c) He was mobbed.

Wicked World Cup question
Who is the only "woman" to have refereed in the World Cup finals?
Wicked answer: Olive Thomas. That's how a misprint in the official FIFA list renamed Welsh referee Clive Thomas!

6 In 1970, the referee had just started the second half of the West Germany v Morocco match when he had to stop it again. Why?

a) He couldn't find his watch.
b) He couldn't find his linesmen.
c) He couldn't find all the players.

7 In the 1982 match against Kuwait, England player Paul Mariner was given a yellow card. What for?

a) Pushing the referee.
b) Shouting at the referee.
c) Kissing the referee.

8 In Italy's 1982 match against Peru, the Italian defender Claudio Gentile was lucky not to have a penalty awarded against him. Why wasn't it?

a) Because the ref was holding his stomach.
b) Because the ref was rubbing his eye.
c) Because the ref was gasping for breath.

9 In the dying minutes of the match against Argentina in 1990, England's John Barnes took a free kick on the edge of the penalty area. What did the referee say to him afterwards?

a) "Bad luck!"
b) "Sorry, sorry!"
c) "What a load of rubbish!"

10 In 1990, Czechoslovakia's Lubomir Moravcik was sent off against Germany. What for?
a) Kicking the ball in the air.
b) Kicking a boot in the air.
c) Kicking a German defender in the air.

Answers:
1 c) That's how referees dressed in 1930. They also wore trousers, which they tucked into their socks.
2 b) But there were no more goals.
3 c) Red and yellow cards had been introduced

in 1970 to avoid confusion where players and referees spoke a different language – but 35 years later confusion still reigned. Graham Poll gave Simunic three yellow cards before realising his mistake and finally sending him off!

4 b) And the second half kicked off as normal.

5 a), b) and **c)**! Thomas had blown his whistle just as the Brazilians had taken a corner. Then they scored, but Thomas refused to allow the goal, and he was mobbed. He pointed out that it was their own fault – the Brazilian winger had delayed taking the corner to have an argument with the linesman about where to put the ball!

6 c) He'd restarted the game without checking that all the players were on the pitch. Some of the Moroccan team were still coming out of the changing room!

7 a) When a pass intended for Mariner got stuck between the ref's feet, the England player hauled him away to get at the ball!

8 a) and **c)** Moments before, the ball had hit the ref in the stomach and winded him. He was still recovering when Gentile committed his foul.

9 b) The referee had positioned himself on the end of the Argentine defender's wall – and Barnes' free kick had hit him!

10 b) It was his own boot! His boot had come off when he was roughly tackled in the Germans' penalty area. When his appeal for a penalty was turned down, Moravcik kicked his boot in the air in disgust. The referee decided this was dissent, so he gave him his second yellow card of the match – and off Moravcik went!

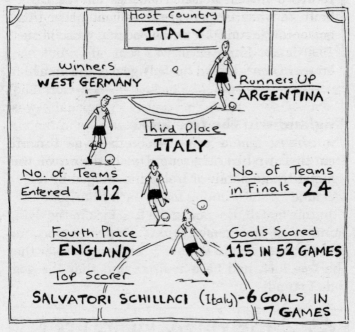

Host Country
ITALY

Winners
WEST GERMANY

Runners Up
ARGENTINA

Third Place
ITALY

No. of Teams
Entered **112**

No. of Teams
in Finals **24**

Fourth Place
ENGLAND

Goals Scored
115 IN 52 GAMES

Top Scorer
SALVATORI SCHILLACI (Italy) - **6 GOALS IN 7 GAMES**

Scotland and England qualified in 1990. For Scotland it was another year of disappointment; for England, even more so but for a different reason.

The Scots yet again failed to survive beyond the first-round group, beating Sweden, but losing to Brazil and – a shock – to Costa Rica in their opening game, 0-1. In some ways that single goal shouldn't have been scored. During a lull in the play, the Costa Rican coach drew a diagram to show one of his forwards, Juan Cayasso, what he wanted to happen. Minutes later, Costa Rica scored – and it was Cayasso who made the goal!

England win the free kicks...

Two draws and a win saw England go through from their first-round group. One of the draws was against the Republic of Ireland, managed by one of England's 1966 winning team, Jack Charlton.

In this match, England got a free kick in the dying minutes of the game. Stuart Pearce stepped up and whacked it into the net ... only to discover that the free kick had been indirect and that the goal didn't stand!

THE THIRTY-MINUTE HERO AWARD...

David O'Leary, Republic of Ireland – who came on for his only appearance as substitute in extra-time during his country's second-round match against Romania. When the match went to a penalty shoot-out it was o'lively O'Leary who hit the winner.

Another free kick decided England's second-round game, against Belgium. Awarded in the last minute of extra time, Paul Gascoigne chipped it forward for David Platt to volley into the net for the winner.

... then pay the penalty!

The quarter-final match against Cameroon also went to extra time – and again it was Lineker to the rescue, converting a couple of penalties to leave England 3-1 winners. They'd reached the semi-final. Germany next!

Wicked World Cup quote
Classic quote from Bobby Robson after England reached the semi-final: "We've got here, but I don't know how."

In the semi-final the penalties went the wrong way. A 1-1 draw after extra time meant a penalty shoot-out. Stuart Pearce and Chris Waddle both missed theirs, and England had lost!

Germany went on to beat Argentina 1-0 in the final. The Argentinians had reached the final with the help of another Maradona handball, this time at the other end of the pitch. In their match against Russia, the referee hadn't seen him stop a Russian shot with his hand!

Wicked fans

The organizers of the 1990 tournament were seriously worried about the hooligans who followed England, so they hit on what they thought was a brilliant solution. They put England's group on the island of Sardinia so that if there was any trouble the fans would be trapped and unable to escape from the police – unless they could swim *really* fast!

Thankfully, very few fans go to matches to cause trouble. Some are a bit on the wicked side, though. So, if you plan to be an international footballer one day, here are the ten most wicked types of supporters to watch out for...

1 The Hair Hauler: When Czechoslovakia went 1-0 up in the 1934 World Cup final against Italy, some Italian fans seized a Czech player's hair through the wire netting surrounding the pitch and only let him free when a rifle-carrying soldier raced to his rescue!

2 The Tomato Tosser: Returning home after coming bottom of their group in 1958, Argentine fans were waiting at the airport to pelt the team with rubbish. The same thing happened to the Italian team in 1966 after their defeat against North Korea.

3 The Bottle Bunger: Brazilian star Garrincha, sent off against home country Chile in 1962, was hit by a bottle as he left the pitch.

4 The Horn Honker: In 1970, a large group of fans spent the night before England's match with Brazil honking their car horns outside their hotel in a bid to keep the players awake.

5 The Souvenir Snatcher: At the end of the 1970 final, Brazilian fans looking for souvenirs stripped their midfield player Tostao. He lost everything except his shorts!

6 The Loo-bag Lobber: Political problems meant that

when the USA played a qualifier for the 1998 competition in Guatemala, the home crowd were not in a good mood. USA goalkeeper Kasey Keller discovered this when he was pelted with plastic bags that the fans had filled up in the loo!

7 The Cheer Chanter: Swedish fans had been whipped up by cheerleaders as their team fought its way to the 1958 final. Then FIFA banned them, the crowd was much quieter – and Sweden lost to Brazil.

8 The Pitch Pouncer: After England had taken the lead in their match against Argentina in 1966, a fan ran onto the pitch – and straight into a punch from the Argentinian left-winger, Oscar Mas.

9 The Game Gambler: An Albanian man wagered his wife on the result of Argentina's match against Romania. He lost the bet – and his wife!

10 The Pedal Pusher: Supporter Clive Tranchant was so anxious to see England play in the 1982 finals that he cycled the 1,000 miles from Sussex to Spain wearing an England shirt and a Union Jack cloak!

Then there are the truly terrible examples of Colombian "fans" in 1994. A few hours before their team's match against the USA, Colombian terrorists faxed their own team selection to the Colombian coach, Francisco Maturana. They warned him that he and the family of Gabriel Gomez, a midfield player, would be blown up if Gomez played. Gomez was left out, and the team lost the match 1-2.

Even worse, one of the USA goals was an own goal by the Colombian defender Andres Escobar. When the team returned home, Escobar was shot dead by an enraged supporter who snarled at him, "thanks for the own goal".

It's not always the fans who cause the players trouble though. Sometimes it's the other way round. In 1954, the Uruguayan players drove their fellow hotel guests mad by continually playing a record at top volume which said how good they were!

1994: BRAZIL'S BRAVES

Host Country
UNITED STATES

Winners
BRAZIL

Runners Up
ITALY

Third Place
SWEDEN

No. of Teams Entered **143**

Fourth Place
BULGARIA

No. of Teams In Finals **24**

Goals Scored
141 IN 52 GAMES

Top Scorer
HRISTO STOICHKOV (Bulgaria) **6 IN 7 GAMES**

England didn't qualify for the 1994 finals. Neither did Northern Ireland. Nor Scotland. Nor Wales! The only United Kingdom "interest" was provided by the Republic of Ireland team managed by England's 1966 World Cup winner Jack Charlton. They managed to fight their way through the first round before being beaten by Netherlands.

Before the tournament began, many people questioned the decision to hold it in America – a country where, in a classic piece of bad counting, a BBC radio commentator said "football is the fourth most popular sport in America," – and went on to give *four* sports that were more popular! "American football, baseball, basketball and ice hockey."

However, although there were some daft incidents – such as 20 American fans walking out of the opening match of the tournament when Germany scored against Bolivia because they thought a match ended once a goal was scored! – crowds were huge and the tournament was a great success.

 THE CROOK-CATCHERS AWARD...

The 1994 World Cup organizers. Before the tournament began the organizers advertised for security staff. Applicants were asked to include a thumbprint along with their details. When these were checked against police files the thumbprints of 57 wanted criminals were discovered!

The biggest sensation was the expulsion of Diego Maradona. After playing brilliantly in Argentina's two opening games, he failed a drugs test and was banned from the rest of the competition. This prompted a fan in Bangladesh to take the FIFA president, Joao Havelange, to court, saying that he'd acted illegally and ruined the World Cup for the 20,000 children in the Bangladesh branch of Maradona's fan club.

The tournament itself was won by Brazil, who beat Italy 0-0 in the final! Yes, for the first time in World Cup history, the winners didn't win the final and the losers didn't lose. Still drawing after extra time, the two teams settled the match on a penalty shoot-out which Brazil won.

Wicked World Cup question

Which 1994 team looked like a herd of elephants until they started playing?

Wicked answer: The champions, Brazil. Before their games the players filed on to the pitch "elephant-style", each of them holding hands with the player in front and the player behind.

Wicked World Cup quotes quiz

With media interest in the 1994 World Cup greater than ever before, there was a truly international crop of wicked quotes. Try to match the quote with the country in this quiz!

Wicked World Cup quote	Country
a) "I do not like for me or my players to be called dogs."	**1** Nigeria
b) "Any player not inspired by that atmosphere should go and play golf with his grandmother."	**2** Germany
c) "Finishing second will be like finishing last."	**3** Rep. Ireland
d) "We're not from the Gobi Desert!"	**4** Colombia
e) "Today, God is…"	**5** USA
f) "I'd say I found the winning scheme. We have ten or even nine players."	**6** Spain
g) "I told my players to run around more and create a draught."	**7** Bulgaria
h) "It's a shame the law allows only two substitutions. Otherwise I would have replaced all eleven players for the second half."	**8** Italy
i) "And the steam has gone completely out of their sails."	**9** Brazil

Answers: a)-5, said a confused Bora Miluthinovic, the USA coach, after a journalist asked him how he felt about his team being considered the underdogs of their group!; b)-1, said Clemens Westerhof, the Nigerian coach, after his team had played Argentina in front of 61,000 spectators; c)-9, said Carlos Alberto Parreira before Brazil's first game. Good job they won the title!; d)-3, said Jack Charlton, the Republic of Ireland manager, when complaining about the Florida heat; e)-7 ... Bulgarian", said Hristo Stoichkov, the Bulgarian striker, after his team had sneaked through to the quarter-finals by beating Mexico in a penalty shoot-out; f)-8, said Arrigo Sacchi, Italy's coach, after his team had lost to the Irish republic with a full team, but beaten Norway after having a player sent off and others injured; g)-2, said Berti Vogts, Germany's coach, when asked what he'd said to his team about playing in the heat; h)-4, said Maturana, the Colombian coach, after their defeat by USA, i)-6, observed TV pundit David Pleat, getting his sayings thoroughly mixed up when talking about Spain.

Kool kit

Perhaps the most startling features of the 1994 competition were the goalkeeper's jerseys. These had been growing more colourful ever since the rule that a goalkeeper could only wear a yellow, green or white jersey was abolished in 1983. Just how colourful they'd become by 1994 can be judged by what Norway's goalkeeper, Erik Thorstvedt, said when he swapped jerseys with his opposite number in the Mexican team, Jorges Campos. Thorstvedt said, "I've been looking for new kitchen curtains for a long time."

Here are a few more wicked facts about World Cup kit:

● After the infamous match between England and Argentina in 1966, England manager Alf Ramsey was so annoyed he ran onto the pitch to stop his right-back George Cohen exchanging shirts with Argentina's Alberto Gonzales.

● Carlos Babington, a late selection for Argentina in 1974, wouldn't have given his blue-and-white striped shirt away anyhow. So delighted was he at being picked for the squad that he slept in it!

● Shirts are important for fans, too. After Germany's fourth World Cup win in 2014, shirt manufacturer Adidas rushed out a replica with an updated four stars above its badge. The shirt was in the shops the day after the final and sold out in hours!

● As for Brazil, champions in 1970, their players wore two shirts each ... well, in their minds anyway. Their manager, Mario Zagalo, would tell the

Brazilian players in team-talks that they must each wear two shirts – a defender's and an attacker's.

● Finally, for a really wicked kit you can't beat a truly dedicated fan ... and Ken Bailey, from Bournemouth, was definitely England's most dedicated fan for many years. He would turn up for games dressed as John Bull – wearing a tailcoat of hunting pink, white breeches, a black top hat and Union Jack waistcoat. As if that wasn't enough, to complete the picture Bailey would be holding a cloth bulldog in his arms!

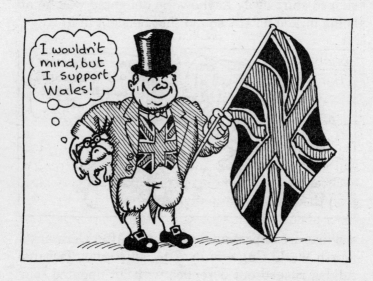

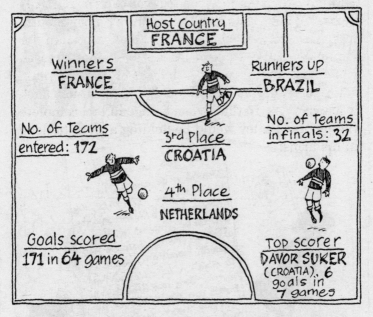

Host Country
FRANCE

Winners
FRANCE

Runners Up
BRAZIL

No. of Teams
entered: 172

3rd Place
CROATIA

No. of Teams
in finals: 32

4th Place
NETHERLANDS

Goals scored
171 in 64 games

TOP scorer
DAVOR SUKER
(CROATIA): 6
goals in
7 games

The 1998 tournament was as wicked as any that had gone before. Scotland's supporters had reason to cheer as their team managed to qualify yet again even though, at one match, they had very little to cheer about – as this supporter's diary reveals…

8 Oct 1996

Och! The Tartan Army are off to Estonia. Not that any of us know where it is. Still, we'll leave no Estonia unturned until we find it.

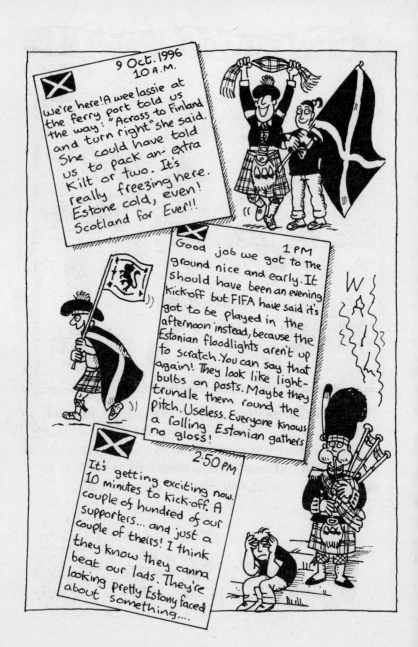

9 Oct. 1996 10 A.M.

We're here! A wee lassie at the ferry port told us the way: "Across to Finland and turn right" she said. She could have told us to pack an extra kilt or two. It's really freezing here. Estone cold, even! Scotland for Ever!!

1 PM

Good job we got to the ground nice and early. It should have been an evening kick-off but FIFA have said it's got to be played in the afternoon instead, because the Estonian floodlights aren't up to scratch. You can say that again! They look like light-bulbs on posts. Maybe they trundle them round the pitch. Useless. Everyone knows a rolling Estonian gathers no gloss!

2.50 PM

It's getting exciting now. 10 minutes to kick-off. A couple of hundred of our supporters... and just a couple of theirs! I think they know they canna beat our lads. They're looking pretty Estony faced about something....

3PM

Here they come! Any minute now! The boys are lining up... The ref's blowing his whistle. We've kicked off..... Come on lads!!

3·01PM

The ref's blown his whistle again. Match abandoned! Estone me!! I wondered where the other team went. Apparently they haven't turned up. They're objecting to FIFA's objecting to their lights. We've come all this way for nothing. Och, it makes you feel like grabbing a bottle of whisky and getting Estoned!

Pheep!

10 oct. 1996

Home again! What a journey. Still, let's look on the bright side. At least I can honestly say I've seen a game in which our lads didna put a foot wrong. What other fan, in the history of the world, can say that?

What happened afterwards was nearly as big a shambles as the original game. The rules said that Scotland should be awarded a 3-0 win, but in the event FIFA changed their minds (and their own rules) and ordered a replay on a neutral ground which ended 0-0. The game took place on 11 February 1997, four months later – making it the longest World Cup game ever played!

In the end it was all in vain. When they reached the finals, Scotland maintained their unenviable record and were knocked out in the first round yet again.

Wicked World Cup question

In 1998 the finals were expanded once more, this time to include 32 teams. These extra places meant that four countries managed to win through to the finals for the first time ever. Which out of this collection were they?

CROATIA   JAMAICA   MOROCCO
    DENMARK   JAPAN
        SAUDI ARABIA
SOUTH AFRICA   TUNISIA

Wicked answer: Croatia, Jamaica, Japan, South Africa. (Denmark first reached the finals in 1986, Morocco in 1970, Saudi Arabia in 1994 and Tunisia in 1978.)

Perilous preliminaries

1998 showed that the path to a World Cup final is pretty perilous for all concerned – teams, fans and non-fans alike...

1 The Maldives, a scattered group of 1,190 islands in the Indian Ocean, set a rotten record in their six matches in the Asian qualifying group:

Won – 0, Drawn – 0, Lost – 6, Goals For – 0, Goals Against – 59, Points 0.

Worst defeat of all? A 17-0 defeat by Iran ... what you might call a Maldives mauling!

2 Then, when the Finals Draw Ceremony took place, one enthusiastic young fan lost out. The ceremony was held at the Stade Vélodrome in France. After an exhibition match ended, the fan ran onto the pitch, dribbled his football close to an empty goal ... only to whack his shot over the bar and into the crowd. Worse still, they wouldn't let him have his ball back!

3 Even non-fans didn't escape. Tickets were in short supply, so when a new batch went on sale, 15 million callers from England alone called the French ticket hot-line. Unfortunately, loads of them forgot to dial the extra digits needed to make a call to France and ended up getting through to poor Maria Pia-Brown, a lady living in Southend!

Those who did get tickets saw plenty of entertaining matches. Reigning champions Brazil powered their way to the final, as did host country France.

In the semi-finals, Brazil had beaten the Netherlands ... who'd beaten Argentina in the round before that ... who, in the round before that, had won what everybody agreed was the match of the tournament...

Argentina v England: red, white – and feeling very blue

It was the match that had everything – except, for England supporters, the right result. Here's the terrific timeline of what happened...

5 minutes, Argentina, playing in blue, take the lead from a penalty.

9 minutes, England, playing in white, equalize - it's another penalty

15 minutes, Michael Owen of England scores a wonder goal. Here's how to do it next time you get a chance in the playground.

* Receive a pass on the centre line. Control it with the outside of your right foot as you start sprinting.

* Outpace the defender who's chasing you - race towards another defender and dribble past him at top speed.

* Then whack the ball into the top corner of the net.

45 minutes, on the stroke of half-time, Argentina draw level.

47 minutes, David Beckham of England is fouled, sees red and kicks out...

....then he sees red again, as the referee sends him off.

83 minutes, Sol Campbell of England scores... but it's disallowed for a foul.

gulp!

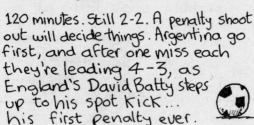
120 minutes. Still 2-2. A penalty shoot out will decide things. Argentina go first, and after one miss each they're leading 4-3, as England's David Batty steps up to his spot kick...
his first penalty ever.

The most wicked World Cup question

...has to be the one posed by TV commentator Brian Moore to ex-England player Kevin Keegan sitting beside him in the commentary box.

Keegan was wrong. Batty missed, England lost the shoot-out 4-3, and were out of the World Cup and feeling blue.

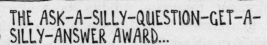

THE ASK-A-SILLY-QUESTION-GET-A-SILLY-ANSWER AWARD...

John Gorman and **Michael Owen**. Before the match, England's assistant manager John Gorman called on the players to avenge Diego Maradona's infamous "Hand of God" goal in 1986. He asked the players where they were that day. "I think I was in my cot, John," replied 18-year-old Michael Owen. Owen was joking. Either that or he still slept in a cot when he was six!

La France fantastique!

The eventual winners in 1998 were host nation France. They'd ridden their luck on the way to the final, needing an extra-time goal in the second round, and to win a penalty shoot-out in the quarter-final. Then, a couple of two-goal stars saw them through.

In the semi-final, France beat Croatia 2-1, with both their goals being scored by wing-back Lilian Thuram – a player who, after injuring his knee as a 16-year-old, had been told by a doctor that he'd never play again. What you might call a wing-back's come-back!

In the final, France's two-goal hero was their midfield maestro Zinedine Zidane. He scored a couple of headers to help his team outplay reigning champions Brazil and win 3-0. That was something of a comeback for Zidane as well – he'd been sent off in an earlier match for stamping on a defender!

Wicked World Cup fact

Zidane's triumph was important for sports equipment company Adidas as well. Before the tournament they'd spent stacks of money making an advert featuring four players who they expected to promote Adidas gear by becoming World Cup stars, only to see three of them sent off: Zidane (France), against South Africa; David Beckham (England) against Argentina; and Patrick Kluivert (the Netherlands) against Belgium. The only one who didn't get a red card was Alessandro Del Piero (Italy) – he was injured and couldn't play!

For fans of France, only one familiar sight was missing from the final. Their giant defender Laurent Blanc didn't feel ready to begin any match unless he'd kissed the bald head of his goalkeeper Fabien Barthez!

It was a superstition that had worked in France's second-round match against Paraguay, because it was Blanc who'd scored the extra-time golden goal to put his country through.

But when it came to the semi-final, Laurent Blanc's luck had run out – he was sent off after a scuffle, and banned from playing in the final.

159

2002: BRAZILIAN BONANZA

Host Countries
KOREAN REPUBLIC and **JAPAN**

winners
BRAZIL

Runners up
GERMANY

Third Place
TURKEY

No. of Teams Entered **199**

Fourth Place
KOREAN REPUBLIC

No. of Teams In Finals **32**

Goals Scored
161 IN **64** GAMES

TOP Scorer
RONALDO (Brazil) – **8 GOALS** IN **7 GAMES**

For the first time, the competition had two host countries, Japan and the Republic of Korea. As they both had to be awarded automatic places as well as title holders France, it meant that there were fewer spots available in the finals. Maybe that's why the qualifying matches were even more wicked than usual...

Wicked Wales

After drawing 1-1 with Ukraine in Kiev, the Welsh team found themselves accused of ball burgling. The Ukranian FA claimed they'd lent the team 12 balls for their pre-match warm-up but only got six back. What's more, they even followed the team to the airport and watched their luggage go through the X-ray machine!

Wicked coaching

After his team weren't supplied with a coach to take them to their training ground, Nigeria's other kind of coach, Jo Bonfrere, got really wild with the Secretary of the Nigerian Football Association, Tijani Yusuf. He said that if his team won their vital qualifying match against Sierra Leone then Yusuf should resign. On the other hand, if they lost then *he* would quit. What happened?

Nigeria lost.

Bonfrere changed his mind and said he'd stay on.

Yusuf had him sacked.

Wembley woes

When both England and their old rivals Germany were drawn in the same qualifying group, memories of the 1966 final came flooding back – especially of Geoff Hurst's hat-trick in the famous 4-2 victory.

They certainly did to England's head coach Kevin Keegan anyway. He promptly told the Germans:

He was joking, of course, but maybe he really should have carried out his threat (even though Hurst was nearly 60!). In the final match ever at the famous Wembley Stadium, England lost 0-1. Afterwards, Keegan had just one more thing to say:

162

Wicked World Cup holiday

Geoff Hurst wasn't at Wembley for that final match. No, he wasn't sulking because Kevin Keegan hadn't picked him. Along with other members of England's 1966 team he was watching the game on a luxury cruise liner's TV. They'd all been given a free cruise in return for talking to the other passengers about their glory days.

After all that, England still managed to qualify for the 2002 finals. In the return match against Germany they found a modern-day Geoff Hurst in striker Michael Owen who scored three goals in a

5-1 win which helped England top the group by goal difference.

Wicked web master

Dutch defender Michael Reiziger tried being wicked before even stepping onto the pitch. He had his own internet website and before Netherland's vital qualifying group match against the Irish Republic wrote that one of his team's tactics should be to annoy Ireland's fiery midfielder Roy Keane and get him sent off.

It didn't work. The match ended 2-2 and guess who ended up leaving the pitch – Reiziger! He was playing so badly his manager substituted him at half-time.

164

Kamikaze Keane

In the end, Roy Keane didn't play in the finals either. That's not to say that the Republic of Ireland didn't qualify – they did. But when the team arrived at their training camp for the finals, Keane began complaining. He didn't like the training pitch, or the facilities, or the travel arrangements, or the amount of time they had to spend talking to the press or, most of all, Ireland's manager Mick McCarthy. The pair had a furious argument and Keane was sent home in disgrace. Without him, Ireland did pretty well! They went through to the next round after finishing second in their group, only to be knocked out by Spain in a penalty shoot-out.

THE SOMETHING FOR NOTHING AWARD...

Roy Keane. The Irish star had already been paid by lemonade makers PepsiCo for allowing them to put his face on millions of drink cans. So for the whole World Cup he was on the shelves but not on the pitch!

Allez-home les Bleus

France, the 1998 World Cup winners, had a terrible tournament. They started off their group matches against little Senegal – and were beaten, 0-1. What made it worse was that most of the Senegal side had spent the season playing for teams in the French League!

France didn't score in their other two games either. They drew 0-0 with Uruguay and lost 0-2 to Denmark. The holders hadn't even reached the second round. Their supporters should have realized the French set-up wasn't as organized as it should have been, though. At the team's last warm-up match before leaving for the tournament every fan had been given a blue scarf reading *"Allez Les Bleus"* (Come on, the Blues!) ... only to discover from the label that it had been made in Italy!

England: Argentine 'appiness then Brazilian blues

Just as they had in 1998, England met Argentina. This time it was a group game – and England gained revenge for their 1998 defeat by winning 1-0. David Beckham ended the match a far happier player this time as well. In 1998 he'd been sent off, but it was his penalty that won the match for England in 2002.

Trevor Sinclair was another player relieved not to have got into trouble – in his case, after the game. Leaving the ground after the match he made the mistake of climbing aboard the coach containing the unhappy Argentine team! "I thought it was a bit quiet," he said.

England didn't last much longer, though. In the quarter-finals they came up against Brazil. After leading 1-0 until just before half-time, they ended up losing 1-2. It was an eventful game for Brazil's Ronaldinho...

• In first-half added time, wriggling Ronny went on a mazy run before passing for teammate Rivaldo to score.

• After five minutes of the second half, rocket Ronny scored with a free-kick from over 30 metres that went over England goalkeeper David Seaman's head.

• Just seven minutes later and it was a case of Ronny red-card as the Brazilian was sent off!

SWEETEST-SMELLING WORLD CUP SHIRT AWARD...

David Beckham, England. When Brazil's star striker Ronaldo swapped shirts with David Beckham after their match he was pleasantly surprised. "Normally when you get shirts they are soaked in sweat and absolutely stink," he said. "But Beckham's shirt smelt only of perfume."

Korean komplaint

Joint-hosts Republic of Korea reached the semi-finals. In the second round they'd beaten Italy 2-1 after extra time. This was a match that had really good news and really bad news for Korea's Ahn Jung-Hwan:

Good News: It was happy Hwan who scored the winning goal.

Bad News: It was ahn-happy Ahn who discovered after the game that he'd been sacked by the president of his club. "I have no intention of paying a salary to someone who has destroyed Italian football!" he ranted – because Ahn's team was Perugia ... of the *Italian* league!

THE SOME PEOPLE ARE NEVER SATISFIED AWARD...

Franz Beckenbauer, ex-World Cup winning player and coach of Germany, who said of the 2002 team: "Apart from Kahn (their goalkeeper) you could put that lot in a bag and beat it with a stick and whoever got hit would deserve it."

And when did he say it? Just after Germany had beaten Republic of Korea to reach the 2002 World Cup final!

Brazilian bonanza

In the final, Brazil and Germany met for the first time ever in the World Cup. Brazil were after another first, too. Never before had a country won every game they'd played.

At half-time, the score was 0-0. Shortly after the restart, Germany hit a post. Brazil swept on to the attack. Midfielder Rivaldo got the ball and tried a long shot. It was a useless one, bobbling along the ground to Franz Beckenbauer's favourite goalkeeper Oliver Kahn ... only for clumsy Kahn to let it bounce out of his hands and straight to Brazilian striker Ronaldo who banged it back into the net!

Not long after, Ronaldo scored again to earn himself the Golden Boot award as the tournament's top goalscorer. It gave Brazil a 2-0 win and the trophy for the fifth time.

THE HOTEL-HELPERS AWARD...

David Beckham, England. Even when the excitement of the World Cup had faded, hotel-keepers still had cause to thank David Beckham. They were flooded with bookings to stay in the same hotel room he'd occupied with England.

Mad Mascots

Fuleco was a big star in 2014. In 2018 it will be the turn of Zabivaka.

So who was Fuleco? Did he fly fabulously around the pitch? Fire fantastic shots from afar? No, footballing Brazilian armadillo Fuleco was the official mascot for the 2014 World Cup.

In 2018 it will be the turn of Russian wolf, Zabivaka. Chosen by the Russian public ahead of a tiger and a cat, Zabivaka is supposedly a fun and skillful little creature who's wanted to be a famous footballer since he was a little ball of fur. Just like a real-life wolf he's full of charm (ask Red Riding Hood) and he always respects his opponents (ask Red Riding Hood's granny!)

What's more, in true footballer-fashion, he just loves posing for photos! Just as well. Zabivaka's image, wearing his trademark super-power sports glasses, will be advertising the tournament everywhere – just as all previous World Cup mascots have done since they first appeared in ... which year?

(a) 1930, in Uruguay

(b) 1966, in England

(c) 1994, in USA

Answer: b) The first official World Cup mascot was an English football-playing lion with flashy red boots called *World Cup Willie*.

On the next page are illustrations of the world cup mascots for every tournament from 1966 to 2018 – except that the order of the mascots has been changed. Can you pair up the mascots with their host countries?

171

172

1 England, 1966; 2 Mexico, 1970; 3 Germany, 1974; 4 Argentina, 1978; 5 Spain, 1982; 6 Mexico, 1986; 7 Italy, 1990; 8 USA, 1994; 9 France, 1998; 10 Korea/Japan, 2002; 11 Germany, 2006; 12 South Africa 2010; 13 Brazil, 2014; 14 Russia, 2018

Answers:

1 j) England 1966 – World Cup Willie

2 f) Mexico 1970 – Juanito

3 a) West Germany 1974 – Tip & Tap

4 e) Argentina 1978 – Gauchito (a gaucho is an Argentinian cowboy)

5 g) Spain 1982 – Naranjito (because the country is famous for its oranges)

6 b) Mexico 1986 – Pique (from 'picante', a hot and spicy Mexican pepper)

7 d) Italy 1990 – Ciao

8 h) United States 1994 – Striker

9 c) France 1998 – Footix

10 k) Korea/Japan 2002 – (L to R) Ato, Kaz and Nik (energy particles. Don't ask me!)

11 m) Germany, 2006 – Gole (a lion) and Pille (a talking football!)

12 i) South Africa, 2010 – Zakumi

13 l) Brazil, 2014 – Fuleco

14 n) Russia, 2018 – (Russian for 'goalscorer)

Host country
GERMANY

winners
ITALY

Runners up
FRANCE

Third Place
GERMANY

NO. of Teams
Entered **194**

NO. of Teams
In Finals **32**

Fourth Place
PORTUGAL

Goals scored
147 IN **64** GAMES

TOP Scorer
MIROSLAV KLOSE (Germany) **5** IN **7** GAMES

In the battle to decide the host country for the 2006 tournament, Germany had been given the vote ahead of England – which meant that England had to qualify, but Germany didn't!

Silence is Goalden

As it happened, England just about made it (but Scotland, Wales and Northern Ireland missed out). It was only after a bad start in their first match against Austria, though. Leading 2-0, they let Austria score two late goals to snatch a draw. England's goalkeeper, David James, got most of the blame after letting the ball slip through his hands for Austria's second goal. Most of the next day's newspapers nicknamed the goalkeeper 'Calamity James', but one preferred to compare him to ... what?

(a) a gorilla
(b) a donkey
(c) a parrot

Answer: b) The disgraceful newspaper even paraded a real donkey and suggested that England coach Sven Goran Eriksson put him in goal for the next match instead.

Eriksson didn't – but he did leave James out. England duly beat Poland 2-1 ... then the players got their own back by refusing to talk to TV and newspaper reporters because of the way David James had been treated.

175

Enter – and exit – the newbies

In 2006 no fewer than eight countries made it to the World Cup finals for the first time. The Czech Republic, Trinidad & Tobago and Serbia & Montenegro were all knocked out in the group stage, but Ukraine got as far as the quarter-final before losing to Italy. The other four newbies were all from Africa. How did they get on? Did they get past the group stage – **Yes or No?**

1. **Angola**, nicknamed The Black Impalas – an impala being a graceful African antelope with extremely sharp horns. So, did Angola get stuck in to their opponents? **Yes or No?**
2. **Ghana**, nicknamed The Black Stars – the star referred to being the one in the middle of their national flag. Was their play out of this world? **Yes or No?**
3. **Côte D'Ivoire (Ivory Coast)**, nicknamed The Elephants! Did they flatten every team that stood in their way? **Yes or No?**
4. **Togo**, nicknamed The Sparrowhawks – a deadly member of the falcon family that preys on

176

other, smaller birds. Does this mean that no country gained 'cheep' wins against Togo! **Yes or No?**

THE CLEAN SHEETS ARE NOT ENOUGH AWARD...

Switzerland – who didn't let a single goal in, but were still knocked out! They topped their group with a goal difference of 4-0, then drew 0-0 with Ukraine in the second round … only to lose the penalty shoot-out. What a Swiss swizz!

I say, I say, I say!

After their silent tactics during qualifying, did England make a big noise when they got to the finals? Well, various people did have a lot to say for themselves. Here's the story of England's World Cup 2006 in their words:

"Getting to the final is the only way I'll see it as a successful tournament. No one comes here to get to the quarter-final and be content with that." – Rio Ferdinand, England's central defender.

Two wins and a draw saw England come top of their group. This was followed by a 1-0 victory over Ecuador in the second round to put England into the quarter-finals and a match against Portugal. Afterwards, would Rio be feeling riotous or rotten? The team's manager had no doubts ...

"It will not be my last day in charge. I'm certain of that. It's not going to go wrong. We will win." – England's manager Sven Goran Eriksson.

It had already been decided that emphatic Eriksson would give up being England's manager once the tournament had ended. In fact his job had already been offered to Portugal's coach Luiz Felipe Scolari – who'd said he didn't want it! Who would win the day? They both knew that England's young striker Wayne Rooney could make the difference ...

"I'm going to try and avoid getting involved with the referee." – England striker, Wayne Rooney.

He didn't manage it. An hour into the match, Rooney reacted badly to a foul by Portugal's Ricardo Carvalho and trod on his opponent's private parts.

As if this wasn't enough, wild Wayne then gave a shove to crafty Cristiano Ronaldo who'd run up to try and persuade the referee to take action. He did. Remorseful Rooney was sent off and England had to battle through the rest of the game with ten men ... which they did! The match, and extra time, ended 0-0. Penalty shoot-out!

Would England punish Portugal? One of the players had been very confident about penalties before the match ...

"We've got dead-ball specialists, some of the best in the world: Steven Gerrard, Frank Lampard, David Beckham. I fancy our chances on penalties, no problems." – England midfielder, Owen Hargreaves.

Unfortunately, Steven Gerrard took a penalty ... and missed. So did Frank Lampard ... and he missed as well. England ended up losing 1-3 on penalties, with their only spot-kick success coming from ... Owen Hargreaves!

 **THE MOST TERRIFYING THREAT AWARD...**
Portugal's goalkeeper, **Ricardo** – who'd said before the game that he'd be willing to do a strip-tease if it would help Portugal win a penalty shoot-out! Maybe that's what put England's penalty-takers off!

The wicked 'What!' quiz

World Cup 2006 had its fair share of wicked happenings – the kind that make you exclaim **'What!'** when you hear about them. Here are the top ten. To discover the full wicked details you have to replace **WHAT!** with one of the following:

angels' voices, ball, being sick, English, hand, heavyweight boxer, highest, net, shorts, spiderman mask, standing, trousers

1 – When England's Joe Cole was injured against Paraguay, referee Marco Rodriguez didn't help matters by **WHAT!** on Cole's **WHAT!**

2 – At a press conference before Croatia's match against Australia, Croatian defender Josip Simunic was told off for talking **WHAT!**

3 – The number of yellow and red cards dished out by referees was the **WHAT!** ever.

4 – When Brazil's striker Ronaldo arrived for his first training session he weighed more than a **WHAT!**

5 – Before being let in to the ground to watch their country play Ivory Coast, hundreds of Netherlands supporters were made to take off their **WHAT!**

6 – After France's match against Togo, French striker Thierry Henry swapped **WHAT!** with Togo's Mohamed Kader.

7 – After scoring a goal against Costa Rica, Ecuador's Ivan Kaviedes pulled a **WHAT!** over his head.

8 – Andre Agassi, ex-Wimbledon tennis champion, offered England some advice, saying: "I think they need to get the **WHAT!** in the **WHAT!** more often."

9 – David Beckham unwittingly appeared in a drinks advertisement which showed him **WHAT!**

10 – France's captain, Zinedine Zidane had retired in

Answers

1 – Standing on his **hand**. After that, Cole needed a **hand** up!

2 – English. His team's officials wanted him to speak in Croatian ... which was pretty tricky for Simunic as he'd been born in Australia!

3 – Highest. 307 yellow cards and 28 red cards were shown to foul footballers. Before that the highest had been 272 yellows (in 2002) and 22 reds (in 1998).

4 – Heavyweight boxer. Ronaldo tipped the scales at 94 kilos, 3 kilos more than the lowest weight for a heavyweight boxer. Even so, he still managed to score 3 goals during the tournament to become the World Cup's record goal scorer with a total of 15.

5 – Trousers – This is because they all carried the name of a Dutch beer company who weren't one of the World Cup's official sponsors.

6 – Shorts. Where will it all end?!

7 – Spiderman mask. Perhaps because he'd made the ball fly into the net!

8 – Ball in the **net**. Good advice, even though it was coming from somebody who'd spent his whole career trying not to put the ball in the net!

9 – Being sick. Beckham had been unwell and threw up during England's match against Ecuador. Drinks maker Gatorade later used the picture in an advert saying how important it was to drink lots of their stuff to stop that sort of embarrassing thing happening.

10 – Angels' voices. France had been doing really badly in the qualifying matches and it's said that Zidane claimed to have heard angels saying that his country needed him!

Angel ... and Demon

Whether or not Zinedine Zidane really did hear the voice of an angel, when he got to the World Cup finals he certainly played like one.

Goals against Spain in the second round and a penalty in a 1-0 win against Portugal in the semi-final saw France reach the final. There they met Italy, looking for their fourth World Cup title.

This definitely was going to be zippy Zidane's last game. Would his career end with the heavenly feeling of holding the world cup? It might have done ... if he hadn't switched from being an angelic player into a demonic fouler. This was the terrible timetable:

7th minute: Materazzi of Italy commits a foul and Zidane scores a penalty to put France 1-0 ahead

19th minute: Materazzi makes up for things by equalising for Italy

90th minute: It's still 1-1, so extra time begins

110th minute: Materazzi and Zidane meet for the last time. As Zidane trots past him, mouthy Materazzi says something nasty. Zidane stops ... turns round ... moves forward ... and head-butts the Italian in the chest! Zidane's career ends with a red card.

120th minute: Penalty shoot-out. Italy had lost all three World Cup penalty shoot-outs they'd played over the years. Could France do it? No. Without Zidane to take one of their kicks, France lost 3-5 to give Italy their fourth World Cup win.

THE BEST PLAYER OF WORLD CUP 2006 AWARD...

Zinedine Zidane. True! This was an official award voted for by journalists. So how did Zidane win? Because the voting took place during the final and had finished before he was sent off! The result couldn't be undone and red-faced officials had to hand the trophy to the red-carded Zidane.

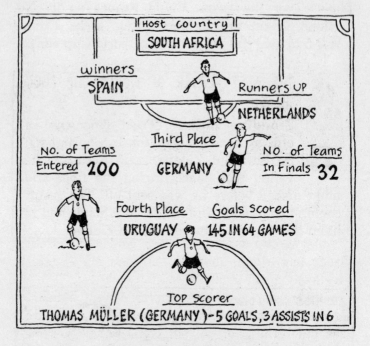

Host Country
SOUTH AFRICA

Winners
SPAIN

Runners Up
NETHERLANDS

Third Place
GERMANY

No. of Teams
Entered 200

No. of Teams
In Finals 32

Fourth Place
URUGUAY

Goals Scored
145 IN 64 GAMES

Top Scorer
THOMAS MÜLLER (GERMANY) – 5 GOALS, 3 ASSISTS IN 6

The 2010 World Cup finals took place in South Africa – the first time that the tournament had ever been held on the African continent.

Unfortunately Northern Ireland, Scotland and Wales failed to qualify. But England made it in style, finishing top of their qualification group. Would they sizzle in South Africa? England's manager, Fabio Capello, thought they could. He said, "I have big confidence in my team."

England supporters certainly thought that Fabio was fab. In December 2009 they voted him Coach

184

of the Year in the BBC's Sports Personality of the Year Awards.

Sadly, that was the only trophy that did come England's way. They had a dreadful time. Here are the lowlights:

• 1st group match v USA: goalkeeper Robert Green lets a long shot slip through his fingers to give away a soft goal. The match ends 1-1.

• 2nd group match v Algeria: a match held at Green Point stadium in Cape Town. As the stadium was partly built on an old golf course, everybody was hoping to see England 'putting' on a great performance! It didn't happen, and the match ended as a 0-0 draw. Algeria were delighted, though. It was the first time they'd ever managed a whole match in the World Cup finals without letting in a goal!

• 3rd group match v Slovenia: a 1-0 win, with England's goal scored by Jermaine Defoe – thanks to Mrs Defoe. The England striker was so excited the night before the game that he needed a phone chat with his mum to calm him down enough to go to sleep.

Sshh! Not so loud! I've only just got him to sleep!

• Round of 16: a 1-4 thumping by old rivals Germany. England are down and out. Only one good thing emerged from the defeat. Finally, after putting up with Germany's moaning about Geoff Hurst's "was it, wasn't it?" goal (see p 86) England had now got a complaint of their own ...

Watch your watch, ref!

England were 1-2 down when midfielder Frank Lampard hammered in a shot which hit Germany's crossbar and bounced down. Ecstatic England appealed for the goal – but the referee said "No"! Had the ball really gone in, though? This time there was no doubt at all. It had. TV replays showed almost instantly that the ball had bounced down a long way behind the goal line.

The dreadful decision finally convinced everybody that goal-line technology – a camera which detects when a goal has been scored – should be brought in. So in 2014 the technology was introduced to the World Cup. When a goal was scored, the referee's watch immediately vibrated and sent him/her a message to say so.

So is that the end of England/Germany goal/no goal arguments? Hopefully. Er ... except for one thing. The 2014 camera system was provided by a company named GoalControl GmbH – from Germany!

Friendless France

France had an even worse time than England – and the whole of the Irish Republic thought it was exactly what they deserved. Why? Because France had beaten their team in a controversial two-legged play-off match. Behind 1-0 after the first leg, Ireland had drawn level in the second leg and taken the match into extra time. Here's what happened next. Try it in your next playground game if you like – but don't expect to have many friends left afterwards!

• Pretend you're French striker Thierry Henry. You're lurking on the left side of the Irish penalty area.

• Now, as the ball whizzes through to you ... stick out your left hand and stop it!

• Then, to make quite sure you've got it under control, use your hand to push it closer to your right foot ...

• Which you use to clip the ball across the goal for somebody pretending to be the French defender William Gallas to head into the net!

• Don't, repeat don't, look in the least bit guilty. Instead, charge off round the pitch in a wild celebration.

THE TERRIBLE CHEAT'S EXCUSE AWARD #2...
Thierry Henry. Unlike Diego Maradona in 1986, terrible Thierry did at least admit that he'd handled the ball. (He couldn't do anything else – millions of TV viewers had seen him do it). But was it his fault that France had beaten Ireland by cheating? Oh, no – it was the referee's! "He should have blown his whistle," said horrible Henry.

If they'd lost a lot of friends in getting to South Africa, France had even fewer by the end. They didn't even like each other! This was their World Cup 2010 record:

1 less striker than they started with, after forward Nicolas Anelka was sent home for insulting manager Raymond Domenech

21 fewer players at next day's training, after they all went on strike in support of Anelka

1 less manager than they started with, after France finished bottom of their group and Domenech resigned

Domenech had the last word, though. In his autobiography he slammed the players for being selfish by referring to a different part of Thierry Henry's anatomy:

"Anelka, Henry – everything revolves around their own belly-buttons."

Paul's predictions

For German fans, one of the stars of the 2010 World Cup had eight legs. An alien footballer? No – an English-born octopus named Paul, living in the Sea Life aquarium in Oberhausen, Germany. His ability to predict Germany's results was uncanny.

Try the method for yourself before your favourite team's next match. If you happen to have a pet octopus it would be handy (or, rather, leggy!) but not essential. Any pet will do. Who knows, maybe your dog, hamster, tortoise or tarantula may be as smart as Paul. This is what to do.

• Get a couple of suitably-sized blocks and stick something to represent the two teams on the front. (Paul's blocks carried Germany's flag and the flag of their opponents.)

• Now pop one of your pet's favourite treats on each of the blocks. (Paul's was a mussel. You might need a couple of bones, nuts, lettuce leaves or flies.)

• Then ... wait to see which of the blocks your pet goes to for its first treat. (If your pet is a tortoise you might have rather a long wait.)

• The chosen block tells you your pet's prediction of which team's going to win the match!

What do you mean it's not a fair test?

During the 2010 World Cup, Germany played seven matches: three group games, a round of 16 match, a quarter-final, a semi-final (against Spain) and a third-place play-off match against Uruguay. Paul predicted the correct result every time!

Yes ... including Germany's defeat by Spain in the semi-final. He wasn't a popular octopus after that one. Quite a few German fans wrote to the newspapers with ideas about the sort of tasty dishes that Paul could be turned into.

On the other tentacle, when he finished with a final, correct prediction that Spain would beat Netherlands in the final, there were calls for him to be given a tank of honour in Madrid Zoo!

Will the clever creature be doing some predicting in 2018? Sadly not. An octopus rarely lives for more than two years and Paul died in October 2010, aged two-and-a-half. He hasn't been forgotten, though. The aquarium erected a memorial in his memory.

Splendid Spain

The 2010 final was held in the Soccer City Stadium in Johannesburg, a ground shaped like a famous African pot known as the calabash. At the end of an intense match it was Spain who lifted the other 'pot' – the World Cup trophy – beating Netherlands 1-0 after extra time.

It was Spain's first-ever triumph. But that was only one of a number of firsts and other records which came their way during the tournament. Try this quick quiz to check out six of the best:

1 Spain were the first team to win the World Cup after – what?
a) finishing second in their group
b) losing a group match to the team they beat in the final
c) losing their opening group match
2 To win the World Cup you need a good defence and a good attack. Spain's record included which of these achievements?

a) keeping clean sheets in all their knockout games
b) setting a record total goal difference for all their 2010 matches
c) scoring fewer goals than any previous winners

3 Spain's match against Netherlands in the final was officially the dirtiest ever. **True or False?**

4 Striker David Villa was the first Spanish player to do what?

a) miss a penalty
b) get sent off
c) take over in goal

5 Andres Iniesta's winning goal for Spain in the final also set a record. Was it...?

a) the longest shot ever
b) the latest ever
c) the first ever headed winner

6 Spain's love-struck goalkeeper Iker Casillas also got himself into the record books. He became the first goalkeeper to give away penalties in two different World Cups. **True or False?**

Answers:

1 c) – a shock 0-1 defeat to Switzerland. After the game, Spain's goalkeeper Iker Casillas was blamed for letting in the goal. He wasn't alone, though. Also blamed by many fans was a female TV reporter named Sara Carbonara, who they thought had been distracting Casillas all through the match by standing behind his goal. How? Because she was also his girlfriend!
2 a) ... **and c)** Spain won each of their 4 knock-out games (Last 16, quarter-final, semi-final and final) 1-0 and conceded only 2 goals all tournament.

192

But they also scored just 8 goals – the fewest ever by any winning team.

3 True. English referee Howard Webb dished out a massive 5 yellows to Spain and further 10 yellows to Netherlands (2 of them adding up to a red for defender John Heitinger).

4 a) – Villa scored both goals in Spain's 2-0 group win over Honduras. The penalty would have given him a hat-trick – but he hit it wide.

5 b) – Amazing Andres scored after 26 minutes of extra time – that is, 116 minutes into the match. (This ignoring the penalty shoot-out goals of 1994 and 2006, of course!)

6 False. Casillas the Cat became the first goalkeeper to save penalties in two world cups when Spain played Paraguay in the 2010 quarter-final. Before that he'd saved a penalty in the 2002 finals against the Republic of Ireland.

Wicked World Cup quote

It was a competition to remember for Netherlands coach Bert Van Marwijk. The fact that his team reached the final showed that his thinking had improved from when the draw for the groups was made at a gathering in December 2009. Then, after the Netherlands had been drawn in the same group as Japan, he'd asked one of their delegation: "Have you seen the Japan coach?" Replied the man he was talking to, Takeshi Okada, "I am the Japan coach!"

Vuvuzela vibrations

One sound above all others dominated the matches in South Africa 2010. It was the long and loud sound of a trumpet-like instrument called a vuvuzela which South African football fans always bring to matches.

How long? Usually for the whole of the match! And how loud? You can judge that by deciding what it was originally used for. Was it a:

a) Meeting-caller

b) Fire alarm

c) Wild animal frightener

Answer: a) The vuvuzela was originally used to call distant villagers to community meetings. In other words, it could be heard miles away! (Which probably meant that it also made a good fire alarm and frightened plenty of wild animals as well!) In fact it was so loud that one manufacturer sold its vuvuzela with a free pack of earplugs!

Unfortunately the instrument was anything but popular outside South Africa. Loads of TV viewers called to complain that they couldn't hear the roar of the crowd and sometimes even the match commentator! If you bought one yourself, don't try to take it to an England game. Following 2010, vuvuzelas are banned at lots of stadiums, including Wembley.

194

The 'Curse of Nike' quiz

Before the 2010 competition began, the sports manufacturer Nike produced a 3-minute long TV commercial featuring five famous players they expected to shine during the tournament. Sadly for them – and the players – it didn't always work out that way. Match the players with their World Cup 2010 (mis)fortunes!

A Fabio Cannavaro (Italy)

1 Broke his elbow before the finals began

B Didier Drogba (Ivory Coast)

2 Failed to score a single goal in four games

C Ronaldinho (Brazil)

3 Announced his retirement before the advert was shown for the first time

D Cristiano Ronaldo (Portugal)

4 Didn't even get to South Africa

E Wayne Rooney (England)

5 Scored just one goal in four games – and that was in a 7-0 win.

B – 1 Drogba broke his elbow in a friendly pre-tournament friendly. He played two-and-a-half group games, but his team didn't reach the knock-out rounds.

C – 4 Ronaldinho watched the advert – and the tournament – from his sofa at home. He wasn't even selected for the Brazilian squad! (He wasn't alone; Theo Walcott of England also had a small part in the advert and he wasn't picked to go to South Africa either).

D – 5 Just one goal in four games was Ronaldo's tally, and that came just 3 minutes from the end of Portugal's 7-0 win over North Korea. They were then beaten by Spain in the first knock-out round.

E – 2 Four games, no goals was Rooney's record.

The tournament wasn't a total disaster for Nike, though. At least they also sponsored the Netherlands team which reached the final and … oh, dear … lost.

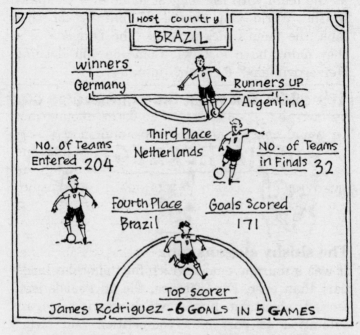

Host country
BRAZIL

winners
Germany

Runners up
Argentina

No. of Teams
Entered 204

Third Place
Netherlands

No. of Teams
in Finals 32

Fourth Place
Brazil

Goals Scored
171

Top scorer
James Rodriguez – 6 GOALS IN 5 GAMES

The 2014 World Cup Finals took place in Brazil – the second time that the tournament had been held there. The first time was in 1950, when England sensationally lost to the USA (see page 46 to remind yourself of the gory details). The England squad was desperately hoping that nothing like the USA disaster would happen again, of course.

But then at least they'd made it to Brazil. Yet again Northern Ireland, Scotland and Wales had failed to qualify for the finals – which meant that they didn't do as well as Bosnia-Herzegovina, who'd won through to the finals for the first time ever.

Although they were knocked out at the group stage the country certainly made their mark in one way: as the team with the longest name ever to appear in the World Cup finals! Thankfully for their fans, the team's nickname is "The Dragons" – so they didn't have to bawl "Come on you Bosnian-Herzegovinians!" for ninety minutes.

The slushy slogans quiz

It was a tournament in which fans played a larger part than ever. For instance, the 32 squads were ferried about in buses which carried slogans submitted as part of a competition and picked by online voting. It was worth entering. The bus makers, the company Hyundai, awarded the authors of the selected slogans one of their cars!

But ... how accurate were the winning slogans? Were they just slushy sentiments, or did they give you an idea of how the team in the bus was going to get on in the tournament? Not for the countries in this quiz they didn't. Here are the slogans for eight of the teams which failed to qualify from their groups. Match each with its hopelessly hopeful bus slogan.

Australia	1. Black Stars: here to illuminate Brazil
Cameroon	2. No one can catch us
England	3. Socceroos: Hopping our way into history!
Ghana	4. Inside our hearts, the passion of a champion
Italy	5. The past is history, the future is victory!
Portugal	6. Let's paint the FIFA World Cup dream blue!
Russia	7. A Lion remains a Lion
Spain	8. The dream of one team, the heartbeat of millions

Answers

Australia – 3: the Socceroos hopped away bottom of their group

Cameroon – 7: the Lions failed to roar and came last in their group

England – 8: the dream turned into a nightmare (as you'll read in a minute!)

Ghana – 1: nicknamed "Black Stars" after their national flag, the team couldn't raise a twinkle and lost every group match

Italy – 6: their slogan was partly right, except that it was the team that felt blue

Portugal – 5: totally wrong … the past was finishing 4th in 2006, the future was coming nowhere in 2014

Russia – 2: well, very few teams were quicker at getting knocked out

Spain – 4: they arrived as champions and went home broken-hearted

199

The heartache of millions

The England team may have dreamed, as their slogan said, but unfortunately their performances gave nothing but heartache to millions – a good few of whom thought that the team bus had been carrying completely the wrong slogan...

Wicked World Cup fact

The team had arrived in Brazil full of hope and with a new manager in charge – Roy Hodgson. He had taken over two years before and led England through a successful qualification campaign.

Brazil 2014 was Hodgson's second World Cup as a manager – but not with England. His first had been as the manager of – which team?

a) Sweden

b) Finland

c) Switzerland

Answer c) He took Switzerland to the finals in 1994 (a year England failed to qualify!)

Roving Roy has held lots of coaching jobs around the world, including a spell in charge of Finland. Although he didn't help them qualify for a major competition, his efforts must have been appreciated, because in 2012 he'd been appointed a **Knight of the Order of the Lion** of Finland for services to football. An official said that during his time as manager he'd "raised the level of Finnish football" – although nobody said by how much!

And there can't have been many managers who can shout at their players in as many languages as Roy Hodgson. He's fluent in English, Swedish, Norwegian, German and Italian – and can make himself understood in Danish, French and Finnish!

Whichever language he did use in 2014, Hodgson wouldn't have had much need for words like 'great', 'wonderful', 'terrific' – or even for a simple word like 'win'. England's performance was awful. Their three group matches ended up like this...

England v Italy – lost 1-2

This match was played at the Arena da Amazônia, a stadium in the Brazilian rainforest where captured water was even used to flush the loos! Unfortunately, England were flushed away too. And, to make matters worse, Italy's winning goal was scored by ex-Manchester City striker, mad Mario Balotelli – a player who'd once set his club house on fire by letting off fireworks in his bathroom!

England v Uruguay – lost 1-2

Yet again, England were undone by a player they should have known all about. Both of Uruguay's goals were scored by Liverpool's Luis Suarez (a man who liked to put plenty of 'bite' in his tackles, as you'll read later). And, for England's players, there was no hiding place during this dismal performance. The match was played at the Arena de São Paulo, a stadium with one of the largest video screens in the world!

England v Costa Rica – drew 0-0

England set a record! They play out their 11th goalless draw in World Cup finals – more than any other country has managed. The match took place at the Estãdio Mineirão, a ground where one of the improvements for the tournament had been to lower the pitch. Not far enough for the England players, though. They played so poorly that they wished the ground would swallow them up!

So, after just three matches, England were on their way home. The only consolation for the players was that at least one member of the party had already beaten them to it...

THE 'HOW NOT TO JUMP FOR JOY' AWARD...
Gary Lewin, England's physiotherapist.
Jumping around in excitement after England had scored in their first match against Italy, Lewin trod on a water bottle and dislocated his ankle. After checking himself and deciding that the injury couldn't be fixed quickly, gloomy Gary had to miss the remaining games. Not all bad news, then.

Mad millions
There was another consolation for England. Well, for the big-wigs of the Football Association, anyway. The prize money. Even though they'd been knocked out at the group stage, England won money simply for reaching the World Cup finals. How much?
- **a)** $80,000
- **b)** $800,000
- **c)** $8,000,000

Answer: c)
Yes, every one of the 16 countries knocked out at the group stage went home with eight million dollars of prize money – even if they'd performed like prize plonkers! So next time you buy your official World Cup souvenir at the supermarket, just remember where a tiddly bit of your pocket money is going to end up!

Here's the rest of the dosh-dispensing list:
- $9 million each: reached last 16
- $14 million each: quarter-finalists

- $20 million: 4th place
- $22 million: 3rd place
- $25 million: runners-up
- $35 million: winners!

Brazilian blues

As the tournament progressed, host nation Brazil made it through to the semi-finals. The slogan on the side of their team bus read, "Brace yourselves! The sixth is coming!". It was referring to the fact that Brazil had won the World Cup five times before, of course. What the slogan's author couldn't possibly have suspected, was that it would be the fans of their semi-final opponents, Germany, who would be shouting it.

After just 30 minutes of the match, Germany were 5-0 ahead. What's more, the sixth goal did come. And the seventh. Germany won the match 7-1, a record score for a World Cup semi-final.

German giants

In the final, Germany met Argentina. For the German defender Christoph Kramer the match was both good news and bad news.

Good news: Kramer wasn't expecting to play. He only came in to the side at the last minute when one of his team suffered a late injury.

Bad news: Kramer lasted only 31 minutes before he had to go off himself. After receiving a nasty crack on the head he'd played on for a while, but the referee advised him to stop. Kramer had been asking him what match he was playing in!

He got the perfect reminder 90 minutes later: a winners' medal. After ending 0-0 at full-time, a goal from Mario Gotze gave Germany a 1-0 victory.

Wicked World Cup fact
2014 was the first time that the World Cup was won by 'Germany'. In 1954, 1974 and 1990 it had been won by 'West Germany' – before the East and West sides of the country reunited.

The '2014 FIRST' quiz

Lots of things happened for the very first time at the last World Cup in Brazil. Each of the following questions start with a number or letter from "2014 FIRST" – how many can you get right?

2 ... the number of games that Spain played before...?
  a) they scored
  b) they were knocked out
  c) they won

0 ... the number of speeches given at the Opening Ceremony. Why?

   a) to save time

   b) no loud speakers

   c) to keep the peace

14 ... the total number of – what? – dotted around the two goals on every pitch?

   a) cameras

   b) ball-boys

   c) advertisements

F ... is for Foam, which was issued to referees for the first time. What did they use it for?

   a) drawing straight lines

   b) drawing triangles

   c) drawing semi-circles

I ... is for In or out? In their group match against Honduras, France appealed to the referee that the ball had crossed Honduras' line and they'd scored. What did the referee do first?

   a) check his watch

   b) listen for voices

   c) look up at the stadium screen

R ... is for Record. What did Germany's striker Miroslav Klose become the first to do?

   a) score 16 goals

   b) score from a corner

   c) score in four World Cups

S ... is for Sweltering. If the temperature went higher then 32°C (90°F) what was the referee allowed to do for the first time?

   a) turn on grass sprinklers

   b) stop the game

   c) call for ice-lollies

T ... is for Teeth: in particular, the teeth owned by Luis Suarez of Uruguay. What did he do for the first time in a World Cup that he'd done twice before?

   a) bite an opponent with them

   b) lose them

   c) get smacked in them

Answers:

2 – b) After losing two games Spain couldn't possibly get through the group stage and became the first World Cup holders to get knocked out that quickly.

0 – c) FIFA's President, Sepp Blatter, was booed the last time he gave a speech. For the first time there were no speeches at the Opening Ceremony.

14 – a) They were for the goal-line technology system, used for the first time in 2014.

F – a) and **c)** For free-kicks, referees used it to mark where players should stand and where the ball should be placed. It was 'vanishing' foam and disappeared a short while after being used.

I – a) Once the new goal-line technology had made its decision the referee would receive a 'goal' or 'no goal' message on a special watch he was wearing.

He might also do **c)** because an animated display would be shown on the stadium's screens for the fans.

R – a) With his goal for Germany in the 7-1 thumping of Brazil, Klose became the all-time highest World Cup goalscorer with 16 goals. It was the fourth World Cup in which he'd scored, but that had been done before by Ronaldo and Pelé (both Brazil).

S – b) 'Cooling periods' were introduced for the first time. If, after 30 minutes had been played, the thermometer showed over 32°C (90°F) the referee could stop the game to let the players cool down.

T – a) During the Uruguay v Italy group match Suarez bit the Italian defender Georgio Chiellini's shoulder. Having done the same thing twice before in league matches, Luis' claim that Chiellini's shoulder hit him in the mouth didn't wash. He was banned for a record nine international matches.

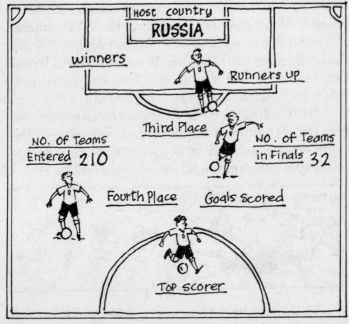

Host Country
RUSSIA

winners

Runners up

Third Place

NO. of Teams
Entered 210

NO. of Teams
in Finals 32

Fourth Place

Goals scored

Top scorer

The 2018 World Cup Finals are taking place in Russia – the first time that the tournament has been held in the eastern part of Europe.

Sadly, both Wales and Northern Ireland failed to qualify again– although they did get closer than usual. Wales had a chance to reach a qualifying play-off. So did Northern Ireland. Unfortunately each had to win their final group match ... and they were playing each other! It was Northern Ireland who came out on top, but they then went on to lose their play-off match to Switzerland.

Scotland didn't qualify again either ... this time thanks to deadly rivals England. The two countries were drawn in the same group and England's 3-0 home win and a 2-2 draw at Hampden Park made all the difference. In the end, that drawn match turned out to be the most exciting game both teams played. Here's how to recreate what happened in the playground with your friends:

1–70 mins Stand around and yawn. Or ask your teacher for extra homework. It'll be more interesting than the first 70 minutes of the match.

70 mins Goal to England! Whoever's pretending to be England forward Alex Oxlade-Chamberlain stops yawning and runs through to score.

71–86 mins More yawning. Whoever's pretending to be the referee should start looking at their watch.

87 mins Excitement! Scotland equalise with a free-kick by Leigh Griffiths.

89 mins Whoever's pretending to be Leigh Griffiths is going to be busy. He scores another free-kick to put Scotland ahead 2-1!

90 mins Get a spare teacher to hold up a board saying there's going to be three minutes of added time.

90 + 2 mins England's Harry Kane scores an equaliser for England! All those playing at being Scots sink to their knees and wail, "I cannae believe it!"

That was one of just two qualifying games that England drew, winning the other eight to qualify easily for Russia 2018.

In charge of the team will be a different manager to Brazil 2014 – former England defender Gareth Southgate.

Southgate is the second manager England have
had since Roy Hodgson departed. He was followed by
Sam Allardyce – who was in charge for just one game!
He resigned after a newspaper suggested that, for a
fat fee, he could be just the person to help anybody
who wanted to find a way around some of the FA's
rules about who's allowed to buy and sell players.
Sadly for Sam, his employers took a dim view of
this – his employers being the FA, of course! Gareth
Southgate stepped in as temporary manager for four
games before being offered the job permanently.

So, how will England get on in Russia with him
in charge? They'll certainly not be expecting much
help if they end up in a penalty shoot-out. Gareth
was in the England team when they faced a shoot-
out against Germany for a place in the final of Euro
2006. With the score at 5-5 each, Southgate stepped
up to take his penalty – and had his feeble shot
saved. Germany scored next to win the shoot-out 6-5.

THE MOTHER KNOWS BEST AWARD...
Gareth Southgate's mum. After seeing
her son's soft penalty saved by the German
goalkeeper she asked him, "Why didn't you
just belt it?"

Still, let's look on the bright side. If England do get involved in a penalty shoot-out at Russia 2018 it will at least mean that they've done better than in 2014 and got past the group stage!

The old faces
Some of the countries which set out to qualify for Russia 2018 have seen it all before. If you've read this book carefully, you won't need to be told the eight previous World Cup champions. Here's the list anyway, together with a 2018 qualifying fact about them. Match the country to the fact.

1. **Argentina**   a) They're hoping to give their opponents a whack with the Kane.
2. **Brazil**   b) They set a record goal difference in qualifying. Champion!
3. **England**   c) They'll be telling their top striker to avoid making any biting tackles.
4. **France**   d) A fabuloso performance saw them unbeaten in qualifying – again.
5. **Germany**   e) They qualified a year early, keeping up their perfect attendance record at World Cup finals.
6. **Italy**   f) They almost made a Messi of their qualifying campaign.
7. **Spain**   g) Their fans will be yelling "Allez les Bleus!" for the 7th time in a row.
8. **Uruguay**   h) Swedes are definitely not their favourite vegetable.

Answers:

1 – f) Argentina, who were struggling until their star player Lionel Messi hit a hat-trick in their final qualifying match to put them through.

2 – e) Brazil had already qualified by mid-2017. They'll be hoping to add another star to the five they already have above their shirt badges, marking their five World Cup victories.

3 – a) England, whose star striker and captain is Harry Kane of Tottenham Hotspur.

4 – g) France, nicknamed "les Bleus" (the Blues). Russia 2018 will be their 7th World Cup finals in succession; they've qualified every time since 1994.

5 – b) Germany, the reigning World Cup champions, who won all ten of their qualifying matches. They banged in 43 goals and only let in four, giving them a goal difference of 39 to set a new record for a European qualifying group.

6 – h) Italy failed to qualify for the finals for the first time in 60 years after losing to Sweden in a play-off.

7 – d) Spain, who won nine and drew one of their ten qualifying matches. They haven't lost a qualifying match since 1993 – a total of 62 games without defeat!

8 – c) Uruguay, whose striker Luis Suarez, was sent off at Brazil 2014 for biting.

Wicked World Cup bloomer

The website of the *Daily Mirror* newspaper got it a bit wrong after the logo for Russia 2018 was officially revealed by three cosmonauts on the International Space Station. The website said they'd been speaking from the International Space Stadium!

First timers

For the first time ever, Russia 2018 saw every single eligible nation enter the competition – all 210 of them. (Just in case you think you can declare your class to be a country, Class8B-land for instance, and enter a team for the 2020 World Cup – you can't. To be eligible you have to have a football association which has paid loads of money to join FIFA.)

Six nations made their debuts. None of them expected to get very far (I don't suppose you'd expect

Class8B-land to reach the finals). They weren't in it to win it, but for the thrill of taking part. So how did they get on?

Sadly **Indonesia** and **Zimbabwe** didn't get on at all ... not even on the pitch! They were both disqualified before the competition began. Why?

a) owing people money   **b)** entry form mistakes

c) interfering governments

Answer:

Indonesia – c) They were disqualified because their government had tried to have clubs removed from the Indonesian league: a bit like the FA demanding that Manchester United and Chelsea be chucked out of the Premier League. (Who said, "What a good idea?") As for **Zimbabwe – a)** They were disqualified because they still hadn't paid their former coach the money they owed him!

As for the other first-time teams:

Gibraltar lost every game in their group, scoring just three goals and conceding 47. It could have been worse. At least their coach, ex-Charlton goalkeeper Jeff Wood, was able to teach them all they needed to know about keeping the score down!

Bhutan were also knocked out at the group stage. But the little land-locked country stuck in the middle of some big mountains – the Himalayas – must have enjoyed their first World Cup matches against the island nation of Sri Lanka. They won 3-1 on aggregate to leave Sri Lanka feeling sea sick.

South Sudan probably couldn't believe what happened in their debut match against Mauritania.

There they are, a little country with regular droughts – and the match is abandoned after ten minutes because of the rain! The score at the time was 1-1, so they were allowed to continue the game from that point the following day. They needn't have bothered; there were no more goals and it ended 1-1.

Kosovo won't be playing in the 2018 finals, either. Although they started out with a 1-1 draw against Finland, they lost the rest of their group games. Even so, it's been a great journey for one of their players. When Kosovo joined FIFA it meant that Norwegian international Valon Berisha could finally play for the country his family came from – and it was Berisha who scored Kosovo's first ever World Cup goal.

Wicked World Cup fact
Myanmar (formerly Burma) had to play all their 2018 home qualifying games at a neutral ground in Thailand. It was punishment for a 2014 qualifying match in which the referee was forced to abandon the game because of objects being thrown on to the pitch when Myanmar were losing.

Why don't they just throw the ref OFF the pitch?

Finally, at Russia 2018 two countries will be making their first ever appearances at a World Cup finals: Panama and Iceland. Will they blow hot or cold? Iceland have already set a record – with a population of just 350,000 they are by far the smallest nation ever to reach the finals. And England won't fancy meeting them, even though its population is 150 times greater. When the two countries met at Euro 2016, Iceland won 2-1!

The numbers game

Once upon a time the only numbers football fans cared about were 1 to 11 – the numbers on the backs of the players' shirts. Nowadays numbers are everywhere.

Here's a collection of statistics about the qualification games for World Cup 2018. Replace each # by a number from this list:

4.3; 4.5; 5; 6; 18; 32; 45; 90; 148; 871; 2018; 2454; 2965

a) There were # qualification matches, spread across # regions.

b) A grand total of # goals were scored altogether.

c) Australia (Oceania) were top group goal scorers, with # goals from # games; Belgium (Europe) had the best goal-scoring average, though, at # goals per game.

d) Referees were busy too, dishing out a total of # yellow cards and # red cards.

e) South America was the dirtiest region, averaging # yellow cards in their # group games.

f) So # countries have now qualified for Russia #. They'll all have high hopes, but # have never got past the group stage!

Answers:

a) There were **871** qualification matches, spread across **6** regions (Africa, Asia, Europe, Oceania, South America and the clunkily-named North, Central America and Caribbean region).

b) A grand total of **2454** goals were scored.

c) Australia (Oceania) were top group goal scorers, with **45** goals from **18** games; Belgium (Europe) had the best goal-scoring average, though, at **4.3** goals per game

d) Referees were busy too, dishing out **2965** yellow cards and **148** red cards. (If the players had scored as many goals as they collected cards the games would have been a lot more exciting!)

e) South America was the dirtiest region, averaging **4.5** yellow cards in their **90** group games.

f). So **32** countries have now qualified for Russia **2018**. They'll all have high hopes, but **5** have never got past the group stage! (Egypt, Iceland, Iran, Panama, Tunisia)

Around the grounds

The 2018 World Cup matches will take place at 12 football grounds dotted around Russia. Just in case you don't live there, or won't be visiting when the tournament's on, here's the next best thing: a funny-fact-finding journey around every one of the World Cup 2018 stadiums!

The opening match of the competition takes place on 14th June at Luzhniki Stadium. It was built in 1956, and is regularly used for athletics. For the World Cup the running track is being removed and extra rows of seating installed for spectators, bringing the total capacity up to 81,000.

Luzhiniki was home to the 1980 Summer Olympic games in Moscow – and a famous controversy. What were the hosts accused of doing whenever one of their javelin throwers was about to perform?

a) shining lights
b) moving markers
c) opening doors

Answer c) They opened huge doors at the end of the stadium, so as to create a helpful tail-wind to help the javelin fly further. The accusation was

Now we're off to Ekaterinburg, Russia's fourth-largest city, for a group match at Ekaterinburg Arena. You can't miss it, at least not from the air. Its roof sticks out all round, so that it looks a bit like a halo. Perhaps we'll see some heavenly football played there! The players could well find the pitch is a bit slippery underfoot, though – the ground was once the home of Russia's speed skating championships.

Kaliningrad Stadium is another ground that is only being used for group matches. It's been built on an area known as Oktyabrsky Island. It'll be interesting to see what happens if the weather turns nasty, because the "island" used to be a swamp and floods very easily. Players here could find themselves swapping their football boots for wellington boots!

Next we're off to Saransk Stadium. Wear sunglasses if you watch a match staged here. The outside of the stadium is coloured orange, red and white! After the tournament is over, the top part of the stadium is being turned into a shopping arcade, so the colourful outside will probably help to attract shoppers. The fourth stadium being used solely for group matches is also unmissable from the outside. Volvograd Stadium has been designed to look a bit like an ice-cream cone with the bottom knocked off. This could be a problem. Volvograd has an average daily temperature of 30°C (85°F) in July – let's hope it doesn't melt in the heat!

The group games are over. We're in to the knockout stage with the round of 16. At this point in the competition the newly-built Rostov Arena hosts its final match. It's situated on the banks of the river Don, and the ripple-covered roof is supposed to look a bit like the waters of the river. Perhaps the football will feature plenty of dribbling, too!

THE ALMOST A BIG BANG AWARD...
Rostov Arena. During the construction of the new stadium some unexploded World War II shells were dug up. There could have been some really explosive matches if they hadn't been found!

The other ground which hosts its final match at the knockout stage is Otkrytiye Arena. Commentators will be pleased to learn that it will be called Spartak Stadium throughout the tournament. It's the home ground of one of Russia's most famous clubs, Moscow Spartak. The most famous athlete shown on TV might be one outside the stadium, rather than in – a huge statue of a legendary gladiator perched on a football. Why? Because "Spartak" comes from the gladiator's name, "Spartacus" (look him up online). The ancient hero was chosen by the club's founders to represent the fighting spirit of their team.

Wicked World Cup fact
The outside of Spartak Stadium can change colour. When Spartak are playing it shows their colours of red and white. If the Russian national team are playing there, it switches to the white, red and dark blue of the Russian flag.

We're in to the quarter final matches now. Four grounds will host them (of course!). Two of them were designed to look really good to a cosmonaut with a telescope – but only one of them will...

The Kazan Arena – designed by the same people as Wembley Stadium – lies beside the Kazanka River. From above, its shape looks like a water lily, which could be confusing for any frog that can jump really high!

The other ground, Fischt Stadium in Sochi no longer looks as good as it did. It hosted the Winter Olympics in 2014 and had a special roof designed for it that looked like the snowy peaks of the nearby Fischt mountain. Sadly it didn't follow FIFA rules – so its roof had to be removed for the World Cup. Local fans are really annoyed. How can their cheering "raise the roof" when it's already been raised!

The other two grounds to be used for the quarter-finals, Nizhny Novgorod Stadium and the Samara Arena had something in common when they were planned. What was it?

a) Volga River **b)** the Kremlin **c)** outer space

Answer

a) Nizhny Novgorod is built on an island at the point where Russia's massive Volga River joins with another river called the Oka.

 THE MOST BORING NAME AWARD...
Nizhny Novgorod, which simply means "lower new town". And even that's no longer true; the town has been there for nearly 800 years!

The Samara Arena was also going to be built on an island in the Volga River – the river is two kilometres wide in the Samara region. The plan was abandoned when somebody pointed out that not only was the island deserted, there was no bridge to it either! The stadium ended up in the city centre.

224

Now we're nearing the climax of the tournament. There are two semi-finals. One of them will take place at Saint Petersburg Stadium, and the players' knees might be really knocking... Because they'll be nervous? Possibly. But it might also be due to the grass moving beneath their boots! Everything is so hi-tech that the pitch can be rolled away beneath the stands so that the stadium can be used for other activities – and, for a while, there were worries that players would feel it shake as they ran on it.

But the stadium in pride of place is Moscow's Luzhniki Stadium. You've already heard that it will be the venue for the opening match. The other semi-final will take place there, as will the World Cup Final itself. "Luzhniki" means "The Meadows", because that's what was there before the arena was built ... and meadows tend to be very wet. That's why the stadium usually has a pitch made from artificial grass. For the World Cup they're going to have to 'turf out' the artificial stuff and lay the real thing!

Hunt the winner

Who will win the 2018 World Cup? Here are some facts to help you decide:

• It's never been won by a country with 8 letters in its name (so bad luck Colombia and Portugal)

• It's never been won by a country with fewer than 5 or more than 11 letters in its name (cheerio Iran and Peru – and Saudi Arabia if you include the space!)

• It's never been won by a country with any of the letters H, J, K, O, Q, V or X in its name (so don't bet on Croatia, Japan, Mexico, Morocco, Poland or South Korea)

• 15 out of the 20 winners have had 5, 6 or 7 letters in its name – which goes up to 18 out of 20 if you count "West Germany" as "Germany". (Aha! ENGLAND has 7 letters in it! Oh dear, BRAZIL has 6.)

• Every single one of the winners has had the letter 'A' in their names. (Aha! ENGLAND has an 'A' in it! Oh dear, and so does BRAZIL.)

Perhaps that's it, then. It might be that the battle for the world cup trophy will be between England and Brazil.

If so, the good news is that England have beaten Brazil to win a World Cup trophy before! On 11th July 1997, that was the outcome of a different type of contest which took place at Sotheby's, the auctioneers in London. There, an anonymous Englishman outbid a Brazilian insurance company to get his hands on the Jules Rimet trophy – the original World Cup, and the one Bobby Moore lifted up high when England won it in 1966.

It cost him £245,000! And it was worth ... £100.

That's because it's not the real solid gold original but a replica, made to put on public exhibition in England to make sure the real thing didn't get stolen.

The bidders knew this. The real Jules Rimet trophy was stolen and melted down, remember, after Brazil won it outright in 1970, but that didn't put them off. The trophy may have been a replica, but it was the only replica in the world, and the winning bidder wanted it that badly.

That's the popularity of the World Cup for you. Wicked!

AUTOGRAPHS

AUTOGRAPHS

AUTOGRAPHS

AUTOGRAPHS

AUTOGRAPHS

AUTOGRAPHS

WANT MORE FOOTBALLING ACTION?

JAMIE JOHNSON

THE Kick Off

Jamie Johnson's got a score to settle

DAN FREEDMAN

"An inspiring read for all football fans" – GARY LINEKER

JAMIE JOHNSON

Shoot To Win

Jamie Johnson's in it to win it

DAN FREEDMAN

JAMIE JOHNSON

It's Jamie Johnson's time to shine

DAN FREEDMAN

JAMIE JOHNSON

Man OF THE Match

It's crunch time for Jamie Johnson

DAN FREEDMAN

"A resounding victory" – **THE TELEGRAPH**

JAMIE JOHNSON

There's only one Jamie Johnson

DAN FREEDMAN

JAMIE JOHNSON

Final Whistle

Jamie Johnson – more than a player

DAN FREEDMAN